ELIZABETH AND HER GERMAN GARDEN

After five years of marriage spent dwelling in a town flat, Elizabeth, made miserable by her urban surroundings, journeys to her husband's country estate in Germany, an ancient former convent surrounded by cornfields and meadows. Instantly captivated by the vast, sprawling wilderness of its garden, Elizabeth makes it her kingdom — and her escape from the humdrum of domesticity and wifehood.

Books by Elizabeth von Arnim
Published by Ulverscroft:

THE SOLITARY SUMMER

ELIZABETH VON ARNIM

ELIZABETH AND HER GERMAN GARDEN

Complete and Unabridged

ULVERSCROFT
Leicester

First published in Great Britain in 1898

This Large Print Edition
published 2016

A catalogue record for this book is available
from the British Library.

ISBN 978–1–4448–2726–2

Published by
F. A. Thorpe (Publishing)
Anstey, Leicestershire

Set by Words & Graphics Ltd.
Anstey, Leicestershire
Printed and bound in Great Britain by
T. J. International Ltd., Padstow, Cornwall

This book is printed on acid-free paper

May 7th. — I love my garden. I am writing in it now in the late afternoon loveliness, much interrupted by the mosquitoes and the temptation to look at all the glories of the new green leaves washed half an hour ago in a cold shower. Two owls are perched near me, and are carrying on a long conversation that I enjoy as much as any warbling of nightingales. The gentleman owl says,

and she answers from her tree a little way off,

beautifully assenting to and completing her lord's remark, as becomes a properly constructed German she-owl. They say the same thing over and over again so emphatically that I think it must be something nasty about me; but I shall not let myself be frightened away by the sarcasm of owls.

This is less a garden than a wilderness. No

one has lived in the house, much less in the garden, for twenty-five years, and it is such a pretty old place that the people who might have lived here and did not, deliberately preferring the horrors of a flat in a town, must have belonged to that vast number of eyeless and earless persons of whom the world seems chiefly composed. Noseless too, though it does not sound pretty; but the greater part of my spring happiness is due to the scent of the wet earth and young leaves.

I am always happy (out of doors be it understood, for indoors there are servants and furniture) but in quite different ways, and my spring happiness bears no resemblance to my summer or autumn happiness, though it is not more intense, and there were days last winter when I danced for sheer joy out in my frost-bound garden, in spite of my years and children. But I did it behind a bush, having a due regard for the decencies.

There are so many bird-cherries round me, great trees with branches sweeping the grass, and they are so wreathed just now with white blossoms and tenderest green that the garden looks like a wedding. I never saw such masses of them; they seemed to fill the place. Even across a little stream that bounds the garden on the east, and right in the middle of the cornfield beyond, there is an immense one, a

2

picture of grace and glory against the cold blue of the spring sky.

My garden is surrounded by cornfields and meadows, and beyond are great stretches of sandy heath and pine forests, and where the forests leave off the bare heath begins again; but the forests are beautiful in their lofty, pink-stemmed vastness, far overhead the crowns of softest gray-green, and underfoot a bright green wortleberry carpet, and everywhere the breathless silence; and the bare heaths are beautiful too, for one can see across them into eternity almost, and to go out on to them with one's face towards the setting sun is like going into the very presence of God.

In the middle of this plain is the oasis of bird-cherries and greenery where I spend my happy days, and in the middle of the oasis is the gray stone house with many gables where I pass my reluctant nights. The house is very old, and has been added to at various times. It was a convent before the Thirty Years' War, and the vaulted chapel, with its brick floor worn by pious peasant knees, is now used as a hall. Gustavus Adolphus and his Swedes passed through more than once, as is duly recorded in archives still preserved, for we are on what was then the high-road between Sweden and Brandenburg the unfortunate.

The Lion of the North was no doubt an estimable person and acted wholly up to his convictions, but he must have sadly upset the peaceful nuns, who were not without convictions of their own, sending them out on to the wide, empty plain to piteously seek some life to replace the life of silence here.

From nearly all the windows of the house I can look out across the plain, with no obstacle in the shape of a hill, right away to a blue line of distant forest, and on the west side uninterruptedly to the setting sun — nothing but a green, rolling plain, with a sharp edge against the sunset. I love those west windows better than any others, and have chosen my bedroom on that side of the house so that even times of hair-brushing may not be entirely lost, and the young woman who attends to such matters has been taught to fulfil her duties about a mistress recumbent in an easychair before an open window, and not to profane with chatter that sweet and solemn time. This girl is grieved at my habit of living almost in the garden, and all her ideas as to the sort of life a respectable German lady should lead have got into a sad muddle since she came to me. The people round about are persuaded that I am, to put it as kindly as possible, exceedingly eccentric, for the news has travelled that I spend the day

4

out of doors with a book, and that no mortal eye has ever yet seen me sew or cook. But why cook when you can get someone to cook for you? And as for sewing, the maids will hem the sheets better and quicker than I could, and all forms of needlework of the fancy order are inventions of the evil one for keeping the foolish from applying their heart to wisdom.

We had been married five years before it struck us that we might as well make use of this place by coming down and living in it. Those five years were spent in a flat in a town, and during their whole interminable length I was perfectly miserable and perfectly healthy, which disposes of the ugly notion that has at times disturbed me that my happiness here is less due to the garden than to a good digestion. And while we were wasting our lives there, here was this dear place with dandelions up to the very door, all the paths grass-grown and completely effaced, in winter so lonely, with nobody but the north wind taking the least notice of it, and in May — in all those five lovely Mays — no one to look at the wonderful bird-cherries and still more wonderful masses of lilacs, everything glowing and blowing, the virginia creeper madder every year, until at last, in October, the very roof was wreathed with blood-red tresses, the owls and the squirrels and all the blessed little birds reigning supreme, and not a living creature ever entering the empty house except the snakes, which got into the habit during those silent years of wriggling up the south wall into the rooms on that side whenever the old housekeeper opened the windows. All that was here, — peace, and happiness, and a reasonable life, — and yet it never struck me to come and live in it. Looking back I am astonished, and can in no way account for the tardiness of my discovery that here, in this far-away corner, was my kingdom of heaven. Indeed, so little did it enter my head to even use the place in summer, that I submitted to weeks of seaside life with all its horrors every year; until at last, in the early spring of last year, having come down for the opening of the village school, and wandering out afterwards into the bare and desolate garden, I don't know what smell of wet earth or rotting leaves brought back my childhood with a rush and all the happy days I had spent in a garden. Shall I ever forget that day? It was the beginning of my real life, my coming of age as it were, and entering into my kingdom. Early March, gray, quiet skies, and brown, quiet earth; leafless and sad and lonely enough out there in the damp and silence, yet there I stood feeling the same rapture of pure delight in the first breath of spring that I used to as a child, and the five wasted years fell from me like a cloak, and the world was full of hope, and I vowed myself then and there to nature, and have been happy ever since.

My other half being indulgent, and with some faint thought perhaps that it might be as well to look after the place, consented to live in it at any rate for a time; whereupon followed six specially blissful weeks from the end of April into June, during which I was here alone, supposed to be superintending the painting and papering, but as a matter of fact only going into the house when the workmen had gone out of it.

How happy I was! I don't remember any time quite so perfect since the days when I was too little to do lessons and was turned out with sugar on my eleven o'clock bread and butter on to a lawn closely strewn with dandelions and daisies. The sugar on the bread and butter has lost its charm, but I love the dandelions and daisies even more passionately now than then, and never would endure to see them all mown away if I were not certain that in a day or two they would be pushing up their little faces again as jauntily as ever. During those six weeks I lived in a world of dandelions and delights. The dandelions carpeted the three lawns, — they used to be lawns, but have long since blossomed out into meadows filled with every sort of pretty weed, — and under and among the groups of leafless oaks and beeches were blue hepaticas, white anemones, violets, and celandines in sheets. The celandines in particular delighted me with their clean, happy brightness, so beautifully trim and newly varnished, as though they too had had the painters at work on them. Then, when the anemones went, came a few stray periwinkles and Solomon's Seal, and all the bird-cherries blossomed in a burst. And then, before I had a little got used to the joy of their flowers against the sky, came the lilacs — masses and masses of them, in clumps on the grass, with other shrubs and trees by the side of walks, and one great continuous bank of them half a mile long right past the west front of the house, away down as far as one could see, shining glorious against a background of firs. When that time came, and when, before it was over, the acacias all blossomed too, and four great clumps of pale, silvery-pink peonies flowered under the south windows, I felt so absolutely happy, and blest, and thankful, and grateful, that I really cannot describe it. My days seemed to melt away in a dream of pink and purple peace.

There were only the old housekeeper and

her handmaiden in the house, so that on the plea of not giving too much trouble I could indulge what my other half calls my *fantaisie dereglee* as regards meals — that is to say, meals so simple that they could be brought out to the lilacs on a tray; and I lived, I remember, on salad and bread and tea the whole time, sometimes a very tiny pigeon appearing at lunch to save me, as the old lady thought, from starvation. Who but a woman could have stood salad for six weeks, even salad sanctified by the presence and scent of the most gorgeous lilac masses? I did, and grew in grace every day, though I have never liked it since. How often now, oppressed by the necessity of assisting at three dining-room meals daily, two of which are conducted by the functionaries held indispensable to a proper maintenance of the family dignity, and all of which are pervaded by joints of meat, how often do I think of my salad days, forty in number, and of the blessedness of being alone as I was then alone!

And then the evenings, when the workmen had all gone and the house was left to emptiness and echoes, and the old house-keeper had gathered up her rheumatic limbs into her bed, and my little room in quite another part of the house had been set ready, how reluctantly I used to leave the friendly frogs and owls, and with my heart somewhere down in my shoes lock the door to the garden behind me, and pass through the long series of echoing south rooms full of shadows and ladders and ghostly pails of painters' mess, and humming a tune to make myself believe I liked it, go rather slowly across the brick-floored hall, up the creaking stairs, down the long whitewashed passage, and with a final rush of panic whisk into my room and double lock and bolt the door!

There were no bells in the house, and I used to take a great dinner-bell to bed with me so that at least I might be able to make a noise if frightened in the night, though what good it would have been I don't know, as there was no one to hear. The housemaid slept in another little cell opening out of mine, and we two were the only living creatures in the great empty west wing. She evidently did not believe in ghosts, for I could hear how she fell asleep immediately after getting into bed; nor do I believe in them, 'mais je les redoute,' as a French lady said, who from her books appears to have been strongminded.

The dinner-bell was a great solace; it was never rung, but it comforted me to see it on the chair beside my bed, as my nights were anything but placid, it was all so strange, and there were such queer creakings and other noises. I used to lie awake for hours, startled out of a light sleep by the cracking of some board, and listen to the indifferent snores of the girl in the next room. In the morning, of course, I was as brave as a lion and much amused at the cold perspirations of the night before; but even the nights seem to me now to have been delightful, and myself like those historic boys who heard a voice in every wind and snatched a fearful joy. I would gladly shiver through them all over again for the sake of the beautiful purity of the house, empty of servants and upholstery.

How pretty the bedrooms looked with nothing in them but their cheerful new papers! Sometimes I would go into those that were finished and build all sorts of castles in the air about their future and their past. Would the nuns who had lived in them know their little white-washed cells again, all gay with delicate flower papers and clean white paint? And how astonished they would be to see cell No. 14 turned into a bathroom, with a bath big enough to insure a cleanliness of body equal to their purity of soul! They would look upon it as a snare of the tempter; and I know that in my own case I only began to be shocked at the blackness of my nails the day that I began to lose the first whiteness of my soul by falling in love at fifteen with the parish organist, or rather with the glimpse of surplice and Roman nose and fiery moustache which was all I ever saw of him, and which I loved to distraction for at least six months; at the end of which time, going out with my governess one day, I passed him in the street, and discovered that his unofficial garb was a frock-coat combined with a turn-down collar and a 'bowler' hat, and never loved him any more.

The first part of that time of blessedness was the most perfect, for I had not a thought of anything but the peace and beauty all round me. Then he appeared suddenly who has a right to appear when and how he will and rebuked me for never having written, and when I told him that I had been literally too happy to think of writing, he seemed to take it as a reflection on himself that I could be happy alone. I took him round the garden along the new paths I had had made, and showed him the acacia and lilac glories, and he said that it was the purest selfishness to enjoy myself when neither he nor the offspring were with me, and that the lilacs wanted thoroughly pruning. I tried to appease him by offering him the whole of my salad and toast supper which stood ready at the foot of the little verandah steps when we came back, but nothing appeased that Man of Wrath, and he said he would go straight back to the neglected family. So he went; and the remainder of the precious time was disturbed by twinges of conscience (to which I am much subject) whenever I found myself wanting to jump for joy. I went to look at the painters every time my feet were for taking me to look at the garden; I trotted diligently up and down the passages; I criticised and suggested and commanded more in one day than I had done in all the rest of the time; I wrote regularly and sent my love; but I could not manage to fret and yearn. What are you to do if your conscience is clear and your liver in order and the sun is shining?

★ ★ ★

May 10th. — I knew nothing whatever last year about gardening and this year know very little more, but I have dawnings of what may be done, and have at least made one great stride — from ipomaea to tea-roses.

The garden was an absolute wilderness. It is all round the house, but the principal part is on the south side and has evidently always been so. The south front is one-storied, a long series of rooms opening one into the other, and the walls are covered with virginia

13

creeper. There is a little verandah in the middle, leading by a flight of rickety wooden steps down into what seems to have been the only spot in the whole place that was ever cared for. This is a semicircle cut into the lawn and edged with privet, and in this semicircle are eleven beds of different sizes bordered with box and arranged round a sun-dial, and the sun-dial is very venerable and moss-grown, and greatly beloved by me. These beds were the only sign of any attempt at gardening to be seen (except a solitary crocus that came up all by itself each spring in the grass, not because it wanted to, but because it could not help it), and these I had sown with ipomaea, the whole eleven, having found a German gardening book, according to which ipomaea in vast quantities was the one thing needful to turn the most hideous desert into a paradise. Nothing else in that book was recommended with anything like the same warmth, and being entirely ignorant of the quantity of seed necessary, I bought ten pounds of it and had it sown not only in the eleven beds but round nearly every tree, and then waited in great agitation for the promised paradise to appear. It did not, and I learned my first lesson.

Luckily I had sown two great patches of sweetpeas which made me very happy all the

summer, and then there were some sunflowers and a few hollyhocks under the south
windows, with Madonna lilies in between.
But the lilies, after being transplanted,
disappeared to my great dismay, for how was
I to know it was the way of lilies? And the
hollyhocks turned out to be rather ugly
colours, so that my first summer was
decorated and beautified solely by sweet-peas.
At present we are only just beginning to
breathe after the bustle of getting new beds
and borders and paths made in time for this
summer. The eleven beds round the sun-dial
are filled with roses, but I see already that I
have made mistakes with some. As I have not
a living soul with whom to hold communion
on this or indeed on any matter, my only way
of learning is by making mistakes. All eleven
were to have been carpeted with purple
pansies, but finding that I had not enough
and that nobody had any to sell me, only six
have got their pansies, the others being sown
with dwarf mignonette. Two of the eleven
are filled with Marie van Houtte roses,
two with Viscountess Folkestone, two with
Laurette Messimy, one with Souvenir de la
Malmaison, one with Adam and Devoniensis,
two with Persian Yellow and Bicolor, and one
big bed behind the sun-dial with three sorts of
red roses (seventy-two in all), Duke of Teck,

Cheshunt Scarlet, and Prefet de Limburg. This bed is, I am sure, a mistake, and several of the others are, I think, but of course I must wait and see, being such an ignorant person. Then I have had two long beds made in the grass on either side of the semicircle, each sown with mignonette, and one filled with Marie van Houtte, and the other with Jules Finger and the Bride; and in a warm corner under the drawing-room windows is a bed of Madame Lambard, Madame de Watteville, and Comtesse Riza du Parc; while farther down the garden, sheltered on the north and west by a group of beeches and lilacs, is another large bed, containing Rubens, Madame Joseph Schwartz, and the Hen. Edith Gifford. All these roses are dwarf; I have only two standards in the whole garden, two Madame George Bruants, and they look like broomsticks. How I long for the day when the tearoses open their buds! Never did I look forward so intensely to anything; and every day I go the rounds, admiring what the dear little things have achieved in the twenty-four hours in the way of new leaf or increase of lovely red shoot.

The hollyhocks and lilies (now flourishing) are still under the south windows in a narrow border on the top of a grass slope, at the foot of which I have sown two long borders of sweetpeas facing the rose beds, so that my roses may have something almost as sweet as themselves to look at until the autumn, when everything is to make place for more tea-roses. The path leading away from this semicircle down the garden is bordered with China roses, white and pink, with here and there a Persian Yellow. I wish now I had put tea-roses there, and I have misgivings as to the effect of the Persian Yellows among the Chinas, for the Chinas are such wee little baby things, and the Persian Yellows look as though they intended to be big bushes.

There is not a creature in all this part of the world who could in the least understand with what heart-beatings I am looking forward to the flowering of these roses, and not a German gardening book that does not relegate all tea-roses to hot-houses, imprisoning them for life, and depriving them for ever of the breath of God. It was no doubt because I was so ignorant that I rushed in where Teutonic angels fear to tread and made my tea-roses face a northern winter; but they did face it under fir branches and leaves, and not one has suffered, and they are looking to-day as happy and as determined to enjoy themselves as any roses, I am sure, in Europe.

★ ★ ★

17

May 14th. — To-day I am writing on the verandah with the three babies, more persistent than mosquitoes, raging round me, and already several of the thirty fingers have been in the ink-pot and the owners consoled when duty pointed to rebukes. But who can rebuke such penitent and drooping sunbonnets? I can see nothing but sunbonnets and pinafores and nimble black legs.

These three, their patient nurse, myself, the gardener, and the gardener's assistant, are the only people who ever go into my garden, but then neither are we ever out of it. The gardener has been here a year and has given me notice regularly on the first of every month, but up to now has been induced to stay on. On the first of this month he came as usual, and with determination written on every feature told me he intended to go in June, and that nothing should alter his decision. I don't think he knows much about gardening, but he can at least dig and water, and some of the things he sows come up, and some of the plants he plants grow, besides which he is the most unflaggingly industrious person I ever saw, and has the great merit of never appearing to take the faintest interest in what we do in the garden. So I have tried to keep him on, not knowing what the next one may be like, and when I asked him what he

18

had to complain of and he replied 'Nothing,' I could only conclude that he has a personal objection to me because of my eccentric preference for plants in groups rather than plants in lines. Perhaps, too, he does not like the extracts from gardening books I read to him sometimes when he is planting or sowing something new. Being so helpless myself, I thought it simpler, instead of explaining, to take the book itself out to him and let him have wisdom at its very source, administering it in doses while he worked. I quite recognise that this must be annoying, and only my anxiety not to lose a whole year through some stupid mistake has given me the courage to do it. I laugh sometimes behind the book at his disgusted face, and wish we could be photographed, so that I may be reminded in twenty years' time, when the garden is a bower of loveliness and I learned in all its ways, of my first happy struggles and failures.

All through April he was putting the perennials we had sown in the autumn into their permanent places, and all through April he went about with a long piece of string making parallel lines down the borders of beautiful exactitude and arranging the poor plants like soldiers at a review. Two long borders were done during my absence one day, and when I explained that I should like the third to have plants in groups and not in lines, and that what I wanted was a natural effect with no bare spaces of earth to be seen, he looked even more gloomily hopeless than usual; and on my going out later on to see the result, I found he had planted two long borders down the sides of a straight walk with little lines of five plants in a row — first five pinks, and next to them five rockets, and behind the rockets five pinks, and behind the pinks five rockets, and so on with different plants of every sort and size down to the end. When I protested, he said he had only carried out my orders and had known it would not look well; so I gave in, and the remaining borders were done after the pattern of the first two, and I will have patience and see how they look this summer, before digging them up again; for it becomes beginners to be humble.

If I could only dig and plant myself! How much easier, besides being so fascinating, to make your own holes exactly where you want them and put in your plants exactly as you choose instead of giving orders that can only be half understood from the moment you depart from the lines laid down by that long piece of string! In the first ecstasy of having a garden all my own, and in my burning impatience to make the waste places blossom

like a rose, I did one warm Sunday in last
year's April during the servants' dinner hour,
doubly secure from the gardener by the day
and the dinner, slink out with a spade and a
rake and feverishly dig a little piece of ground
and break it up and sow surreptitious
ipomaea, and run back very hot and guilty
into the house, and get into a chair and
behind a book and look languid just in time
to save my reputation. And why not? It is not
graceful, and it makes one hot; but it is a
blessed sort of work, and if Eve had had
a spade in Paradise and known what to do
with it, we should not have had all that sad
business of the apple.

What a happy woman I am living in a
garden, with books, babies, birds, and
flowers, and plenty of leisure to enjoy them!
Yet my town acquaintances look upon it as
imprisonment, and burying, and I don't know
what besides, and would rend the air with
their shrieks if condemned to such a life.
Sometimes I feel as if I were blest above all
my fellows in being able to find my happiness
so easily. I believe I should always be good if
the sun always shone, and could enjoy myself
very well in Siberia on a fine day. And what
can life in town offer in the way of pleasure to
equal the delight of any one of the calm
evenings I have had this month sitting alone

at the foot of the verandah steps, with the perfume of young larches all about, and the May moon hanging low over the beeches, and the beautiful silence made only more profound in its peace by the croaking of distant frogs and hooting of owls? A cockchafer darting by close to my ear with a loud hum sends a shiver through me, partly of pleasure at the reminder of past summers, and partly of fear lest he should get caught in my hair. The Man of Wrath says they are pernicious creatures and should be killed. I would rather get the killing done at the end of the summer and not crush them out of such a pretty world at the very beginning of all the fun.

This has been quite an eventful afternoon. My eldest baby, born in April, is five years old, and the youngest, born in June, is three; so that the discerning will at once be able to guess the age of the remaining middle or May baby. While I was stooping over a group of hollyhocks planted on the top of the only thing in the shape of a hill the garden possesses, the April baby, who had been sitting pensive on a tree stump close by, got up suddenly and began to run aimlessly about, shrieking and wringing her hands with every symptom of terror. I stared, wondering what had come to her; and then I saw that a whole army of young cows, pasturing in a field next to the garden, had got through the hedge and were grazing perilously near my tea-roses and most precious belongings. The nurse and I managed to chase them away, but not before they had trampled down a border of pinks and lilies in the cruellest way, and made great holes in a bed of China roses, and even begun to nibble at a Jackmanni clematis that I am trying to persuade to climb up a tree trunk. The gloomy gardener happened to be ill in bed, and the assistant was at vespers — as Lutheran Germany calls afternoon tea or its equivalent — so the nurse filled up the holes as well as she could with mould, burying the crushed and mangled roses, cheated for ever of their hopes of summer glory, and I stood by looking on dejectedly. The June baby, who is two feet square and valiant beyond her size and years, seized a stick much bigger than herself and went after the cows, the cowherd being nowhere to be seen. She planted herself in front of them brandishing her stick, and they stood in a row and stared at her in great astonishment; and she kept them off until one of the men from the farm arrived with a whip, and having found the cowherd sleeping peacefully in the shade, gave him a sound beating. The cowherd is a great hulking young man, much bigger than the man who beat him, but he took his punishment as part of the day's work and made no remark of any sort. It could not have hurt him much through his leather breeches, and I think he deserved it; but it must be demoralising work for a strong young man with no brains looking after cows. Nobody with less imagination than a poet ought to take it up as a profession.

After the June baby and I had been welcomed back by the other two with as many hugs as though we had been restored to them from great perils, and while we were peacefully drinking tea under a beech tree, I happened to look up into its mazy green, and there, on a branch quite close to my head, sat a little baby owl. I got on the seat and caught it easily, for it could not fly, and how it had reached the branch at all is a mystery. It is a little round ball of gray fluff, with the quaintest, wisest, solemn face. Poor thing! I ought to have let it go, but the temptation to keep it until the Man of Wrath, at present on a journey, has seen it was not to be resisted, as he has often said how much he would like to have a young owl and try and tame it. So I put it into a roomy cage and slung it up on a branch near where it had been sitting, and which cannot be far from its nest and its mother. We had hardly subsided again to our tea when I saw two more balls of fluff on the ground in the long grass and scarcely distinguishable at a little distance from small mole-hills. These were promptly united to their relation in the cage, and now when the Man of Wrath comes home, not only shall he be welcomed by a wife decked with the orthodox smiles, but by the three little longed-for owls. Only it seems wicked to take them from their mother, and I know that I shall let them go again some day — perhaps the very next time the Man of Wrath goes on a journey. I put a small pot of water in the cage, though they never could have tasted water yet unless they drink the raindrops off the beech leaves. I suppose they get all the liquid they need from the bodies of the mice and other dainties provided for them by their fond parents. But the raindrop idea is prettier.

★   ★   ★

May 15th. — How cruel it was of me to put those poor little owls into a cage even for one night! I cannot forgive myself, and shall never pander to the Man of Wrath's wishes again. This morning I got up early to see how they were getting on, and I found the door of the cage wide open and no owls to be seen. I thought of course that somebody had stolen them — some boy from the village, or perhaps the chastised cowherd. But looking about I saw one perched high up in the branches of the beech tree, and then to my dismay one lying dead on the ground. The third was nowhere to be seen, and is probably safe in its nest. The parents must have torn at the bars of the cage until by chance they got the door open, and then dragged the little ones out and up into the tree. The one that is dead must have been blown off the branch, as it was a windy night and its neck is broken. There is one happy life less in the garden to-day through my fault, and it is such a lovely, warm day — just the sort of weather for young soft things to enjoy and grow in. The babies are greatly distressed, and are digging a grave, and preparing funeral wreaths of dandelions.

Just as I had written that I heard sounds of arrival, and running out I breathlessly told the Man of Wrath how nearly I had been able to give him the owls he has so often said he would like to have, and how sorry I was they were gone, and how grievous the death of one, and so on after the voluble manner of women.

He listened till I paused to breathe, and then he said, 'I am surprised at such cruelty.

How could you make the mother owl suffer so? She had never done you any harm.'

Which sent me out of the house and into the garden more convinced than ever that he sang true who sang —

Two paradises 'twere in one to live in Paradise alone.

★ ★ ★

May 16th. — The garden is the place I go to for refuge and shelter, not the house. In the house are duties and annoyances, servants to exhort and admonish, furniture, and meals; but out there blessings crowd round me at every step — it is there that I am sorry for the unkindness in me, for those selfish thoughts that are so much worse than they feel; it is there that all my sins and silliness are forgiven, there that I feel protected and at home, and every flower and weed is a friend and every tree a lover. When I have been vexed I run out to them for comfort, and when I have been angry without just cause, it is there that I find absolution. Did ever a woman have so many friends? And always the same, always ready to welcome me and fill me with cheerful thoughts. Happy children of a common Father, why should I, their own sister, be less content and joyous than they? Even in a thunder storm, when other people are running into the house, I run out of it. I do not like thunder storms — they frighten me for hours before they come, because I always feel them on the way; but it is odd that I should go for shelter to the garden. I feel better there, more taken care of, more petted. When it thunders, the April baby says, 'There's lieber Gott scolding those angels again.' And once, when there was a storm in the night, she complained loudly, and wanted to know why lieber Gott didn't do the scolding in the daytime, as she had been so tight asleep. They all three speak a wonderful mixture of German and English, adulterating the purity of their native tongue by putting in English words in the middle of a German sentence. It always reminds me of Justice tempered by Mercy. We have been cowslipping to-day in a little wood dignified by the name of the Hirschwald, because it is the happy hunting-ground of innumerable deer who fight there in the autumn evenings, calling each other out to combat with bayings that ring through the silence and send agreeable shivers through the lonely listener. I often walk there in September, late in the evening, and sitting on a fallen tree listen fascinated to their angry cries.

We made cowslip balls sitting on the grass. The babies had never seen such things nor had imagined anything half so sweet. The Hirschwald is a little open wood of silver birches and springy turf starred with flowers, and there is a tiny stream meandering amiably about it and decking itself in June with yellow flags. I have dreams of having a little cottage built there, with the daisies up to the door, and no path of any sort — just big enough to hold myself and one baby inside and a purple clematis outside. Two rooms — a bedroom and a kitchen. How scared we would be at night, and how completely happy by day! I know the exact spot where it should stand, facing south-east, so that we should get all the cheerfulness of the morning, and close to the stream, so that we might wash our plates among the flags. Sometimes, when in the mood for society, we would invite the remaining babies to tea and entertain them with wild strawberries on plates of horse-chestnut leaves; but no one less innocent and easily pleased than a baby would be permitted to darken the effulgence of our sunny cottage — indeed, I don't suppose that anybody wiser would care to come. Wise people want so many things before they can even begin to enjoy themselves, and I feel perpetually apologetic when with them, for only being able to offer them that which I love best myself — apologetic, and ashamed of being so easily contented.

The other day at a dinner party in the nearest town (it took us the whole afternoon to get there) the women after dinner were curious to know how I had endured the winter, cut off from everybody and snowed up sometimes for weeks.

'Ah, these husbands!' sighed an ample lady, lugubriously shaking her head; 'they shut up their wives because it suits them, and don't care what their sufferings are.'

Then the others sighed and shook their heads too, for the ample lady was a great local potentate, and one began to tell how another dreadful husband had brought his young wife into the country and had kept her there, concealing her beauty and accomplishments from the public in a most cruel manner, and how, after spending a certain number of years in alternately weeping and producing progeny, she had quite lately run away with somebody unspeakable — I think it was the footman, or the baker, or someone of that sort.

'But I am quite happy,' I began, as soon as I could put in a word.

'Ah, a good little wife, making the best of it,' and the female potentate patted my hand, but continued gloomily to shake her head.

'You cannot possibly be happy in the winter entirely alone,' asserted another lady, the wife of a high military authority and not accustomed to be contradicted.

'But I am.'

'But how can you possibly be at your age? No, it is not possible.'

'But I *am*.'

'Your husband ought to bring you to town in the winter.'

'But I don't want to be brought to town.'

'And not let you waste your best years buried.'

'But I like being buried.'

'Such solitude is not right.'

'But I'm not solitary.'

'And can come to no good.' She was getting quite angry.

There was a chorus of No Indeeds at her last remark, and renewed shaking of heads.

'I enjoyed the winter immensely,' I persisted when they were a little quieter; 'I sleighed and skated, and then there were the children, and shelves and shelves full of — ' I was going to say books, but stopped. Reading is an occupation for men; for women it is reprehensible waste of time. And how could I talk to them of the happiness I felt when the sun shone on the snow, or of the deep delight of hoar-frost days?

'It is entirely my doing that we have come down here,' I proceeded, 'and my husband only did it to please me.'

'Such a good little wife,' repeated the patronising potentate, again patting my hand with an air of understanding all about it, 'really an excellent little wife. But you must not let your husband have his own way too much, my dear, and take my advice and insist on his bringing you to town next winter.' And then they fell to talking about their cooks, having settled to their entire satisfaction that my fate was probably lying in wait for me too, lurking perhaps at that very moment behind the apparently harmless brass buttons of the man in the hall with my cloak.

I laughed on the way home, and I laughed again for sheer satisfaction when we reached the garden and drove between the quiet trees to the pretty old house; and when I went into the library, with its four windows open to the moonlight and the scent, and looked round at the familiar bookshelves, and could hear no sounds but sounds of peace, and knew that here I might read or dream or idle exactly as I chose with never a creature to disturb me, how grateful I felt to the kindly Fate that has brought me here and given me a heart to understand my own blessedness, and rescued me from a life like that I had just seen — a life spent with the odours of other people's dinners in one's nostrils, and the noise of their wrangling servants in one's ears, and parties and tattle for all amusement.

But I must confess to having felt sometimes quite crushed when some grand person, examining the details of my home through her eyeglass, and coolly dissecting all that I so much prize from the convenient distance of the open window, has finished up by expressing sympathy with my loneliness, and on my protesting that I like it, has murmured, 'sehr anspruchslos.' Then indeed I have felt ashamed of the fewness of my wants; but only for a moment, and only under the withering influence of the eyeglass; for, after all, the owner's spirit is the same spirit as that which dwells in my servants — girls whose one idea of happiness is to live in a town where there are others of their sort with whom to drink beer and dance on Sunday afternoons. The passion for being for ever with one's fellows, and the fear of being left for a few hours alone, is to me wholly incomprehensible. I can entertain myself quite well for weeks together, hardly aware, except for the pervading peace, that I have been alone at all. Not but what I like to have people staying with me for a few days, or even for a few weeks, should they be as anspruchslos as I am myself, and content with simple joys; only, any one who comes here and would be happy must have something in him; if he be a mere blank creature, empty of head and heart, he will very probably find it dull. I should like my house to be often full if I could find people capable of enjoying themselves. They should be welcomed and sped with equal heartiness; for truth compels me to confess that, though it pleases me to see them come, it pleases me just as much to see them go.

On some very specially divine days, like today, I have actually longed for someone else to be here to enjoy the beauty with me. There has been rain in the night, and the whole garden seems to be singing — not the untiring birds only, but the vigorous plants, the happy grass and trees, the lilac bushes — oh, those lilac bushes! They are all out to-day, and the garden is drenched with the scent. I have brought in armfuls, the picking is such a delight, and every pot and bowl and tub in the house is filled with purple glory, and the servants think there is going to be a party and are extra nimble, and I go from room to room gazing at the sweetness, and the windows are all flung open so as to join the scent within to the scent without; and the servants gradually discover that there is no party, and wonder why the house should be filled with flowers for one woman by herself, and I long more and more for a kindred spirit — it seems so greedy to have so much loveliness to oneself — but kindred spirits are so very, very rare; I might almost as well cry for the moon. It is true that my garden is full of friends, only they are — dumb.

★　★　★

June 3rd. — This is such an out-of-the-way corner of the world that it requires quite unusual energy to get here at all, and I am thus delivered from casual callers; while, on the other hand, people I love, or people who love me, which is much the same thing, are not likely to be deterred from coming by the roundabout train journey and the long drive at the end. Not the least of my many blessings is that we have only one neighbour. If you have to have neighbours at all, it is at least a mercy that there should be only one; for with people dropping in at all hours and wanting to talk to you, how are you to get on with your life, I should like to know, and read your books, and dream your dreams to your satisfaction? Besides, there is always the certainty that either you or the dropper-in will say something that would have been better left unsaid, and I have a holy horror of gossip and mischief-making. A woman's tongue is a deadly weapon and the most difficult thing in the world to keep in order, and things slip off it with a facility nothing short of appalling at the very moment when it ought to be most quiet. In such cases the only safe course is to talk steadily about cooks and children, and to pray that the visit may not be too prolonged, for if it is you are lost. Cooks I have found to be the best of all subjects — the most phlegmatic flush into life at the mere word, and the joys and sufferings connected with them are experiences common to us all.

Luckily, our neighbour and his wife are both busy and charming, with a whole troop of flaxenhaired little children to keep them occupied, besides the business of their large estate. Our intercourse is arranged on lines of the most beautiful simplicity. I call on her once a year, and she returns the call a fortnight later; they ask us to dinner in the summer, and we ask them to dinner in the winter. By strictly keeping to this, we avoid all danger of that closer friendship which is only another name for frequent quarrels. She is a pattern of what a German country lady should be, and is not only a pretty woman but an energetic and practical one, and the combination is, to say the least, effective. She is up at daylight superintending the feeding of the stock, the butter-making, the sending off of the milk for sale; a thousand things get done while most people are fast asleep, and before lazy folk are well at breakfast she is off in her pony-carriage to the other farms on the place, to rate the 'mamsells,' as the head women are called, to poke into every corner, lift the lids off the saucepans, count the new-laid eggs, and box, if necessary, any careless dairymaid's ears. We are allowed by law to administer 'slight corporal punishment' to our servants, it being left entirely to individual taste to decide what 'slight' shall be, and my neighbour really seems to enjoy using this privilege, judging from the way she talks about it. I would give much to be able to peep through a keyhole and see the dauntless little lady, terrible in her wrath and dignity, standing on tiptoe to box the ears of some great strapping girl big enough to eat her.

The making of cheese and butter and sausages *excellently* well is a work which requires brains, and is, to my thinking, a very admirable form of activity, and entirely worthy of the attention of the intelligent. That my neighbour is intelligent is at once made evident by the bright alertness of her eyes — eyes that nothing escapes, and that only gain in prettiness by being used to some good purpose. She is a recognised authority for miles around on the mysteries of sausage-making, the care of calves, and the slaughtering of swine; and with all her manifold duties and daily prolonged absences from home, her children are patterns of health and neatness, and of what dear little German children, with white pigtails and fearless eyes and thick legs, should be. Who shall say that such a life is sordid and dull and unworthy of a high order of intelligence? I protest that to me it is a beautiful life, full of wholesome outdoor work, and with no room for those listless moments of depression and boredom, and of wondering what you will do next, that leave wrinkles round a pretty woman's eyes, and are not unknown even to the most brilliant. But while admiring my neighbour, I don't think I shall ever try to follow in her steps, my talents not being of the energetic and organising variety, but rather of that order which makes their owner almost lamentably prone to take up a volume of poetry and wander out to where the kingcups grow, and, sitting on a willow trunk beside a little stream, forget the very existence of everything but green pastures and still waters, and the glad blowing of the wind across the joyous fields. And it would make me perfectly wretched to be confronted by ears so refractory as to require boxing.

Sometimes callers from a distance invade my solitude, and it is on these occasions that I realise how absolutely alone each individual is, and how far away from his neighbour; and while they talk (generally about babies, past, present, and to come), I fall to wondering at the vast and impassable distance that separates one's own soul from the soul of the person sitting in the next chair. I am speaking of comparative strangers, people who are forced to stay a certain time by the eccentricities of trains, and in whose presence you grope about after common interests and shrink back into your shell on finding that you have none. Then a frost slowly settles down on me and I grow each minute more benumbed and speechless, and the babies feel the frost in the air and look vacant, and the callers go through the usual form of wondering who they most take after, generally settling the question by saying that the May baby, who is the beauty, is like her father, and that the two more or less plain ones are the image of me, and this decision, though I know it of old and am sure it is coming, never fails to depress me as much as though I heard it for the first time. The babies are very little and inoffensive and good, and it is hard that they should be used as a means of filling up gaps in conversation, and their features pulled to pieces one by one, and all their weak points noted and criticised, while they stand smiling shyly in the operator's face, their very smile drawing forth comments on the shape of their mouths; but, after all, it does not occur very often, and they are one of those few interests one has in common with other people, as everybody seems to have babies. A garden, I have discovered, is by no means a fruitful topic, and it is amazing how few persons really love theirs — they all pretend they do, but you can hear by the very tone of their voice what a lukewarm affection it is. About June their interest is at its warmest, nourished by agreeable supplies of strawberries and roses; but on reflection I don't know a single person within twenty miles who really cares for his garden, or has discovered the treasures of happiness that are buried in it, and are to be found if sought for diligently, and if needs be with tears. It is after these rare calls that I experience the only moments of depression from which I ever suffer, and then I am angry at myself, a well-nourished person, for allowing even a single precious hour of life to be spoilt by anything so indifferent. That is the worst of being fed enough, and clothed enough, and warmed enough, and of having everything you can reasonably desire — on the least provocation you are made uncomfortable and unhappy by such abstract discomforts as being shut out from a nearer approach to your neighbour's soul; which is on the face of it foolish, the probability being that he hasn't got one.

The rockets are all out. The gardener, in a fit of inspiration, put them right along the very front of two borders, and I don't know what his feelings can be now that they are all flowering and the plants behind are completely hidden; but I have learned another lesson, and no future gardener shall be allowed to run riot among my rockets in quite so reckless a fashion. They are charming things, as delicate in colour as in scent, and a bowl of them on my writing-table fills the room with fragrance. Single rows, however, are a mistake; I had masses of them planted in the grass, and these show how lovely they can be. A border full of rockets, mauve and white, and nothing else, must be beautiful; but I don't know how long they last nor what they look like when they have done flowering. This I shall find out in a week or two, I suppose. Was ever a would-be gardener left so entirely to his own blundering? No doubt it would be a gain of years to the garden if I were not forced to learn solely by my failures, and if I had some kind creature to tell me when to do things. At present the only flowers in the garden are the rockets, the pansies in the rose beds, and two groups of azaleas — mollis and pontica. The azaleas have been and still are gorgeous; I only planted them this spring and they almost at once began to flower, and the sheltered corner they are in looks as though it were filled with imprisoned and perpetual sunsets. Orange, lemon, pink in every delicate shade — what they will be next year and in succeeding years when the bushes are bigger, I can imagine from the way they have begun life. On gray, dull days the effect is absolutely startling. Next autumn I shall make a great bank of them in front of a belt of fir trees in rather a gloomy nook. My tea-roses are covered with buds which will not open for at least another week, so I conclude this is not the sort of climate where they will flower from the very beginning of June to November, as they are said to do.

★ ★ ★

July 11th. — There has been no rain since the day before Whitsunday, five weeks ago, which partly, but not entirely, accounts for the disappointment my beds have been. The dejected gardener went mad soon after Whitsuntide, and had to be sent to an

42

asylum. He took to going about with a spade in one hand and a revolver in the other, explaining that he felt safer that way, and we bore it quite patiently, as becomes civilised beings who respect each other's prejudices, until one day, when I mildly asked him to tie up a fallen creeper — and after he bought the revolver my tones in addressing him were of the mildest, and I quite left off reading to him aloud — he turned round, looked me straight in the face for the first time since he has been here, and said, 'Do I look like Graf X — (a great local celebrity), or like a monkey?' After which there was nothing for it but to get him into an asylum as expeditiously as possible. There was no gardener to be had in his place, and I have only just succeeded in getting one; so that what with the drought, and the neglect, and the gardener's madness, and my blunders, the garden is in a sad condition; but even in a sad condition it is the dearest place in the world, and all my mistakes only make me more determined to persevere.

The long borders, where the rockets were, are looking dreadful. The rockets have done flowering, and, after the manner of rockets: in other walks of life, have degenerated into sticks; and nothing else in those borders intends to bloom this summer. The giant poppies I had planted out in them in April have either died off or remained quite small, and so have the columbines; here and there a delphinium droops unwillingly, and that is all. I suppose poppies cannot stand being moved, or perhaps they were not watered enough at the time of transplanting; anyhow, those borders are going to be sown to-morrow with more poppies for next year; for poppies I will have, whether they like it or not, and they shall not be touched, only thinned out.

Well, it is no use being grieved, and after all, directly I come out and sit under the trees, and look at the dappled sky, and see the sunshine on the cornfields away on the plain, all the disappointment smooths itself out, and it seems impossible to be sad and discontented when everything about me is so radiant and kind.

To-day is Sunday, and the garden is so quiet, that, sitting here in this shady corner watching the lazy shadows stretching themselves across the grass, and listening to the rooks quarrelling in the treetops, I almost expect to hear English church bells ringing for the afternoon service. But the church is three miles off, has no bells, and no afternoon service. Once a fortnight we go to morning prayer at eleven and sit up in a sort of private box with a room behind, whither we can retire unobserved when the sermon is too long or our flesh too weak, and hear ourselves being prayed for by the blackrobed parson. In winter the church is bitterly cold; it is not heated, and we sit muffled up in more furs than ever we wear out of doors; but it would of course be very wicked for the parson to wear furs, however cold he may be, so he puts on a great many extra coats under his gown, and, as the winter progresses, swells to a prodigious size. We know when spring is coming by the reduction in his figure. The congregation sit at ease while the parson does the praying for them, and while they are droning the long-drawn-out chorales, he retires into a little wooden box just big enough to hold him. He does not come out until he thinks we have sung enough, nor do we stop until his appearance gives us the signal. I have often thought how dreadful it would be if he fell ill in his box and left us to go on singing. I am sure we should never dare to stop, unauthorised by the Church. I asked him once what he did in there; he looked very shocked at such a profane question, and made an evasive reply.

If it were not for the garden, a German Sunday would be a terrible day; but in the garden on that day there is a sigh of relief and more profound peace, nobody raking or sweeping or fidgeting; only the little flowers themselves and the whispering trees.

I have been much afflicted again lately by visitors — not stray callers to be got rid of after a due administration of tea and things you are sorry afterwards that you said, but people staying in the house and not to be got rid of at all. All June was lost to me in this way, and it was from first to last a radiant month of heat and beauty; but a garden where you meet the people you saw at breakfast, and will see again at lunch and dinner, is not a place to be happy in. Besides, they had a knack of finding out my favourite seats and lounging in them just when I longed to lounge myself; and they took books out of the library with them, and left them face downwards on the seats all night to get well drenched with dew, though they might have known that what is meat for roses is poison for books; and they gave me to understand that if they had had the arranging of the garden it would have been finished long ago — whereas I don't believe a garden ever is finished. They have all gone now, thank heaven, except one, so that I have a little breathing space before others begin to arrive. It seems that the place interests people, and that there is a sort of novelty in staying in such a deserted corner of the world, for they were in a perpetual state of mild amusement at being here at all. Irais is the only one left. She is a young woman with a beautiful, refined face, and her eyes and straight, fine eyebrows are particularly lovable. At meals she dips her bread into the salt-cellar, bites a bit off, and repeats the process, although providence (taking my shape) has caused salt-spoons to be placed at convenient intervals down the table. She lunched to-day on beer, Schweine-koteletten, and cabbage-salad with caraway seeds in it, and now I hear her through the open window, extemporising touching melodies in her charming, cooing voice. She is thin, frail, intelligent, and lovable, all on the above diet. What better proof can be needed to establish the superiority of the Teuton than the fact that after such meals he can produce such music? Cabbage salad is a horrid invention, but I don't doubt its utility as a means of encouraging thoughtfulness; nor will I quarrel with it, since it results so poetically, any more than I quarrel with the manure that results in roses, and I give it to Irais every day to make her sing. She is the sweetest singer I have ever heard, and has a charming trick of making up songs as she goes along. When she begins, I go and lean out of the window and look at my little friends out there in the borders while listening to her music, and feel full of pleasant sadness and regret. It is so sweet to be sad when one has nothing to be sad about.

The April baby came panting up just as I had written that, the others hurrying along behind, and with flaming cheeks displayed for my admiration three brand-new kittens, lean and blind, that she was carrying in her pinafore, and that had just been found motherless in the woodshed.

'Look,' she cried breathlessly, 'such a much!'

I was glad it was only kittens this time, for she had been once before this afternoon on purpose, as she informed me, sitting herself down on the grass at my feet, to ask about the lieber Gott, it being Sunday and her pious little nurse's conversation having run, as it seems, on heaven and angels.

Her questions about the lieber Gott are better left unrecorded, and I was relieved when she began about the angels.

'What do they wear for clothes?' she asked in her German-English.

'Why, you've seen them in pictures,' I answered, 'in beautiful, long dresses, and with big, white wings.'

'Feathers?' she asked.

'I suppose so, — and long dresses, all white and beautiful.'

'Are they girlies?'

'Girls? Ye — es.'

'Don't boys go into the Himmel?'

'Yes, of course, if they're good.'

'And then what do *they* wear?' 'Why, the same as all the other angels, I suppose.'

'Dwesses?'

She began to laugh, looking at me sideways as though she suspected me of making jokes. 'What a funny Mummy!' she said, evidently much amused. She has a fat little laugh that is very infectious.

'I think,' said I, gravely, 'you had better go and play with the other babies.'

She did not answer, and sat still a moment watching the clouds. I began writing again.

'Mummy,' she said presently.

'Well?'

'Where do the angels get their dwesses?'

I hesitated. 'From lieber Gott,' I said.

'Are there shops in the Himmel?'

'Shops? No.'

'But, then, where does lieber Gott buy their dwesses?'

'Now run away like a good baby; I'm busy.'

'But you said yesterday, when I asked about lieber Gott, that you would tell about Him on Sunday, and it is Sunday. Tell me a story about Him.'

There was nothing for it but resignation, so I put down my pencil with a sigh. 'Call the others, then.'

She ran away, and presently they all three emerged from the bushes one after the other, and tried all together to scramble on to my knee. The April baby got the knee as she always seems to get everything, and the other two had to sit on the grass.

I began about Adam and Eve, with an eye to future parsonic probings. The April baby's eyes opened wider and wider, and her face grew redder and redder. I was surprised at the breathless interest she took in the story — the other two were tearing up tufts of grass and hardly listening. I had scarcely got to the angels with the flaming swords and announced that that was all, when she burst out, 'Now I'll tell about it. Once upon a time there was Adam and Eva, and they had plenty of clothes, and there was no snake, and lieber Gott wasn't angry with them, and they could eat as many apples as they liked, and was happy for ever and ever — there now!'

She began to jump up and down defiantly on my knee.

'But that's not the story,' I said rather helplessly. 'Yes, yes! It's a much nicelier one! Now another.'

'But these stories are true,' I said severely; 'and it's no use my telling them if you make them up your own way afterwards.'

'Another! another!' she shrieked, jumping

up and down with redoubled energy, all her silvery curls flying.

I began about Noah and the flood.

'Did it rain so badly?' she asked with a face of the deepest concern and interest.

'Yes, all day long and all night long for weeks and weeks — '

'And was everybody so wet?'

'Yes — '

'But why didn't they open their umbwellas?'

Just then I saw the nurse coming out with the tea-tray.

'I'll tell you the rest another time,' I said, putting her off my knee, greatly relieved; 'you must all go to Anna now and have tea.'

'I don't like Anna,' remarked the June baby, not having hitherto opened her lips; 'she is a stupid girl.'

The other two stood transfixed with horror at this statement, for, besides being naturally extremely polite, and at all times anxious not to hurt any one's feelings, they had been brought up to love and respect their kind little nurse.

The April baby recovered her speech first, and lifting her finger, pointed it at the criminal in just indignation. 'Such a child will never go into the Himmel,' she said with great emphasis, and the air of one who delivers judgment.

September 15th. — This is the month of quiet days, crimson creepers, and blackberries; of mellow afternoons in the ripening garden; of tea under the acacias instead of the too shady beeches; of wood-fires in the library in the chilly evenings. The babies go out in the afternoon and blackberry in the hedges; the three kittens, grown big and fat, sit cleaning themselves on the sunny verandah steps; the Man of Wrath shoots partridges across the distant stubble; and the summer seems as though it would dream on for ever. It is hard to believe that in three months we shall probably be snowed up and certainly be cold. There is a feeling about this month that reminds me of March and the early days of April, when spring is still hesitating on the threshold and the garden holds its breath in expectation. There is the same mildness in the air, and the sky and grass have the same look as then; but the leaves tell a different tale, and the reddening creeper on the house is rapidly approaching its last and loveliest glory.

My roses have behaved as well on the whole as was to be expected, and the Viscountess Folkestones and Laurette Messimys have been most beautiful, the latter being quite the loveliest things in the garden, each flower an exquisite loose cluster of coral-pink petals, paling at the base to a yellow-white. I have ordered a hundred standard tea-roses for planting next month, half of which are Viscountess Folkestones, because the tea-roses have such a way of hanging their little heads that one has to kneel down to be able to see them well in the dwarf forms — not but what I entirely approve of kneeling before such perfect beauty, only it dirties one's clothes. So I am going to put standards down each side of the walk under the south windows, and shall have the flowers on a convenient level for worship. My only fear is, that they will stand the winter less well than the dwarf sorts, being so difficult to pack up snugly. The Persian Yellows and Bicolors have been, as I predicted, a mistake among the tea-roses; they only flower twice in the season and all the rest of the time look dull and moping; and then the Persian Yellows have such an odd smell and so many insects inside them eating them up. I have ordered Safrano tea-roses to put in their place, as they all come out next month and are to be grouped in the grass; and the semicircle being immediately under the windows, besides having the best position in the place, must be reserved solely for my choicest treasures. I have had a great many disappointments, but feel as though

I were really beginning to learn. Humility, and the most patient perseverance, seem almost as necessary in gardening as rain and sunshine, and every failure must be used as a stepping-stone to something better.

I had a visitor last week who knows a great deal about gardening and has had much practical experience. When I heard he was coming, I felt I wanted to put my arms right round my garden and hide it from him; but what was my surprise and delight when he said, after having gone all over it, 'Well, I think you have done wonders.' Dear me, how pleased I was! It was so entirely unexpected, and such a complete novelty after the remarks I have been listening to all the summer. I could have hugged that discerning and indulgent critic, able to look beyond the result to the intention, and appreciating the difficulties of every kind that had been in the way. After that I opened my heart to him, and listened reverently to all he had to say, and treasured up his kind and encouraging advice, and wished he could stay here a whole year and help me through the seasons. But he went, as people one likes always do go, and he was the only guest I have had whose departure made me sorry.

The people I love are always somewhere else and not able to come to me, while I can at any time fill the house with visitors about whom I know little and care less. Perhaps, if I saw more of those absent ones, I would not love them so well — at least, that is what I think on wet days when the wind is howling round the house and all nature is overcome with grief; and it has actually happened once or twice when great friends have been staying with me that I have wished, when they left, I might not see them again for at least ten years. I suppose the fact is, that no friendship can stand the breakfast test, and here, in the country, we invariably think it our duty to appear at breakfast. Civilisation has done away with curl-papers, yet at that hour the soul of the Hausfrau is as tightly screwed up in them as was ever her grandmother's hair; and though my body comes down mechanically, having been trained that way by punctual parents, my soul never thinks of beginning to wake up for other people till lunch-time, and never does so completely till it has been taken out of doors and aired in the sunshine. Who can begin conventional amiability the first thing in the morning? It is the hour of savage instincts and natural tendencies; it is the triumph of the Disagreeable and the Cross. I am convinced that the Muses and the Graces never thought of having breakfast anywhere but in bed.

November 11th. — When the gray November weather came, and hung its soft dark clouds low and unbroken over the brown of the ploughed fields and the vivid emerald of the stretches of winter corn, the heavy stillness weighed my heart down to a forlorn yearning after the pleasant things of childhood, the petting, the comforting, the warming faith in the unfailing wisdom of elders. A great need of something to lean on, and a great weariness of independence and responsibility took possession of my soul; and looking round for support and comfort in that transitory mood, the emptiness of the present and the blankness of the future sent me back to the past with all its ghosts. Why should I not go and see the place where I was born, and where I lived so long; the place where I was so magnificently happy, so exquisitely wretched, so close to heaven, so near to hell, always either up on a cloud of glory, or down in the depths with the waters of despair closing over my head? Cousins live in it now, distant cousins, loved with the exact measure of love usually bestowed on cousins who reign in one's stead; cousins of practical views, who have dug up the flower-beds and planted cabbages where roses grew; and though through all the years since my father's death I have held my head so high that it hurt, and loftily refused to listen to their repeated suggestions that I should revisit my old home, something in the sad listlessness of the November days sent my spirit back to old times with a persistency that would not be set aside, and I woke from my musings surprised to find myself sick with longing. It is foolish but natural to quarrel with one's cousins, and especially foolish and natural when they have done nothing, and are mere victims of chance. Is it their fault that my not being a boy placed the shoes I should otherwise have stepped into at their disposal? I know it is not; but their blamelessness does not make me love them more. 'Noch ein dummes Frauenzimmer!' cried my father, on my arrival into the world — he had three of them already, and I was his last hope, — and a dummes Frauenzimmer I have remained ever since; and that is why for years I would have no dealings with the cousins in possession, and that is why, the other day, overcome by the tender influence of the weather, the purely sentimental longing to join hands again with my childhood was enough to send all my pride to the winds, and to start me off without warning and without invitation on my pilgrimage.

I have always had a liking for pilgrimages, and if I had lived in the Middle Ages would have spent most of my time on the way to Rome. The pilgrims, leaving all their cares at home, the anxieties of their riches or their debts, the wife that worried and the children that disturbed, took only their sins with them, and turning their backs on their obligations, set out with that sole burden, and perhaps a cheerful heart. How cheerful my heart would have been, starting on a fine morning, with the smell of the spring in my nostrils, fortified by the approval of those left behind, accompanied by the pious blessings of my family, with every step getting farther from the suffocation of daily duties, out into the wide fresh world, out into the glorious free world, so poor, so penitent, and so happy! My dream, even now, is to walk for weeks with some friend that I love, leisurely wandering from place to place, with no route arranged and no object in view, with liberty to go on all day or to linger all day, as we choose; but the question of luggage, unknown to the simple pilgrim, is one of the rocks on which my plans have been shipwrecked, and the other is the certain censure of relatives, who, not fond of walking themselves, and having no taste for noonday naps under hedges, would be sure to paralyse my plans before they had grown to maturity by the honest horror of their cry, 'How very unpleasant if you were to meet any one you know!' The relative of five hundred years back would simply have said, 'How holy!'

My father had the same liking for pilgrimages — indeed, it is evident that I have it from him — and he encouraged it in me when I was little, taking me with him on his pious journeys to places he had lived in as a boy. Often have we been together to the school he was at in Brandenburg, and spent pleasant days wandering about the old town on the edge of one of those lakes that lie in a chain in that wide green plain; and often have we been in Potsdam, where he was quartered as a lieutenant, the Potsdam pilgrimage including hours in the woods around and in the gardens of Sans Souci, with the second volume of Carlyle's Frederick under my father's arm; and often did we spend long summer days at the house in the Mark, at the head of the same blue chain of lakes, where his mother spent her young years, and where, though it belonged to cousins, like everything else that was worth having, we could wander about as we chose, for it was empty, and sit in the deep windows of rooms where there was no furniture, and the painted Venuses and cupids on the ceiling still smiled irrelevantly and stretched their futile wreaths above the emptiness beneath. And while we sat and rested, my father told me, as my grandmother had a hundred times told him, all that had happened in those rooms in the far-off days when people danced and sang and laughed through life, and nobody seemed ever to be old or sorry.

There was, and still is, an inn within a stone's throw of the great iron gates, with two very old lime trees in front of it, where we used to lunch on our arrival at a little table spread with a red and blue check cloth, the lime blossoms dropping into our soup, and the bees humming in the scented shadows overhead. I have a picture of the house by my side as I write, done from the lake in old times, with a boat full of ladies in hoops and powder in the foreground, and a youth playing a guitar. The pilgrimages to this place were those I loved the best.

But the stories my father told me, sometimes odd enough stories to tell a little girl, as we wandered about the echoing rooms, or hung over the stone balustrade and fed the fishes in the lake, or picked the pale dog-roses in the hedges, or lay in the boat in a shady reed-grown bay while he smoked to keep the mosquitoes off, were after all only traditions, imparted to me in small doses from time to time, when his earnest desire not to raise his remarks above the level of dulness supposed to be wholesome for Backfische was neutralised by an impulse to share his thoughts with somebody who would laugh; whereas the place I was bound for on my latest pilgrimage was filled with living, first-hand memories of all the enchanted years that lie between two and eighteen. How enchanted those years are is made more and more clear to me the older I grow. There has been nothing in the least like them since; and though I have forgotten most of what happened six months ago, every incident, almost every day of those wonderful long years is perfectly distinct in my memory.

But I had been stiffnecked, proud, unpleasant, altogether cousinly in my behaviour towards the people in possession. The invitations to revisit the old home had ceased. The cousins had grown tired of refusals, and had left me alone. I did not even know who lived in it now, it was so long since I had had any news. For two days I fought against the strong desire to go there that had suddenly seized me, and assured myself that I would not go, that it would be absurd to go, undignified, sentimental, and silly, that I did not know them and would be in an awkward position, and that I was old enough to know better. But who can foretell from one hour to the next what a woman will do? And when does she ever know better? On the third morning I set out as hopefully as though it were the most natural thing in the world to fall unexpectedly upon hitherto consistently neglected cousins, and expect to be received with open arms.

It was a complicated journey, and lasted several hours. During the first part, when it was still dark, I glowed with enthusiasm, with the spirit of adventure, with delight at the prospect of so soon seeing the loved place again; and thought with wonder of the long years I had allowed to pass since last I was there. Of what I should say to the cousins, and of how I should introduce myself into their midst, I did not think at all: the pilgrim spirit was upon me, the unpractical spirit that takes no thought for anything, but simply wanders along enjoying its own emotions. It was a quiet, sad morning, and there was a thick mist. By the time I was in the little train on the light railway that passed through the village nearest my old home, I had got over my first enthusiasm, and had entered the stage of critically examining the changes that had been made in the last ten years. It was so misty that I could see nothing of the familiar country from the carriage windows, only the ghosts of pines in the front row of the forests;

but the railway itself was a new departure, unknown in our day, when we used to drive over ten miles of deep, sandy forest roads to and from the station, and although most people would have called it an evident and great improvement, it was an innovation due, no doubt, to the zeal and energy of the reigning cousin; and who was he, thought I, that he should require more conveniences than my father had found needful? It was no use my telling myself that in my father's time the era of light railways had not dawned, and that if it had, we should have done our utmost to secure one; the thought of my cousin, stepping into my shoes, and then altering them, was odious to me. By the time I was walking up the hill from the station I had got over this feeling too, and had entered a third stage of wondering uneasily what in the world I should do next. Where was the intrepid courage with which I had started? At the top of the first hill I sat down to consider this question in detail, for I was very near the house now, and felt I wanted time. Where, indeed, was the courage and joy of the morning? It had vanished so completely that I could only suppose that it must be lunch time, the observations of years having led to the discovery that the higher sentiments and virtues fly affrighted on the approach of lunch, and none fly quicker than courage. So I ate the lunch I had brought with me, hoping that it was what I wanted; but it was chilly, made up of sandwiches and pears, and it had to be eaten under a tree at the edge of a field; and it was November, and the mist was thicker than ever and very wet — the grass was wet with it, the gaunt tree was wet with it, I was wet with it, and the sandwiches were wet with it. Nobody's spirits can keep up under such conditions; and as I ate the soaked sandwiches, I deplored the headlong courage more with each mouthful that had torn me from a warm, dry home where I was appreciated, and had brought me first to the damp tree in the damp field, and when I had finished my lunch and dessert of cold pears, was going to drag me into the midst of a circle of unprepared and astonished cousins. Vast sheep loomed through the mist a few yards off. The sheep dog kept up a perpetual, irritating yap. In the fog I could hardly tell where I was, though I knew I must have played there a hundred times as a child. After the fashion of woman directly she is not perfectly warm and perfectly comfortable, I began to consider the uncertainty of human life, and to shake my head in gloomy approval as lugubrious lines of pessimistic poetry suggested themselves to my mind.

Now it is clearly a desirable plan, if you want to do anything, to do it in the way consecrated by custom, more especially if you are a woman. The rattle of a carriage along the road just behind me, and the fact that I started and turned suddenly hot, drove this truth home to my soul. The mist hid me, and the carriage, no doubt full of cousins, drove on in the direction of the house; but what an absurd position I was in! Suppose the kindly mist had lifted, and revealed me lunching in the wet on their property, the cousin of the short and lofty letters, the unangenehme Elisabeth! 'Die war doch immer verdreht,' I could imagine them hastily muttering to each other, before advancing wreathed in welcoming smiles. It gave me a great shock, this narrow escape, and I got on to my feet quickly, and burying the remains of my lunch under the gigantic molehill on which I had been sitting, asked myself nervously what I proposed to do next. Should I walk back to the village, go to the Gasthof, write a letter craving permission to call on my cousins, and wait there till an answer came? It would be a discreet and sober course to pursue; the next best thing to having written before leaving home. But the Gasthof of a north German village is a dreadful place, and the remembrance of one in which I had taken refuge once from a thunderstorm was still so vivid that nature itself cried out against this plan. The mist, if anything, was growing denser. I knew every path and gate in the place. What if I gave up all hope of seeing the house, and went through the little door in the wall at the bottom of the garden, and confined myself for this once to that? In such weather I would be able to wander round as I pleased, without the least risk of being seen by or meeting any cousins, and it was after all the garden that lay nearest my heart. What a delight it would be to creep into it unobserved, and revisit all the corners I so well remembered, and slip out again and get away safely without any need of explanations, assurances, protestations, displays of affection, without any need, in a word, of that exhausting form of conversation, so dear to relations, known as Redensarten! The mist tempted me. I think if it had been a fine day I would have gone soberly to the Gasthof and written the conciliatory letter; but the temptation was too great, it was altogether irresistible, and in ten minutes I had found the gate, opened it with some difficulty, and was standing with a beating heart in the garden of my childhood.

Now I wonder whether I shall ever again feel thrills of the same potency as those that ran through me at that moment. First of all I was trespassing, which is in itself thrilling; but how much more thrilling when you are trespassing on what might just as well have been your own ground, on what actually was for years your own ground, and when you are in deadly peril of seeing the rightful owners, whom you have never met, but with whom you have quarrelled, appear round the corner, and of hearing them remark with an inquiring and awful politeness 'I do not think I have the pleasure — ?' Then the place was unchanged. I was standing in the same mysterious tangle of damp little paths that had always been just there; they curled away on either side among the shrubs, with the brown tracks of recent footsteps in the centre of their green stains, just as they did in my day. The overgrown lilac bushes still met above my head. The moisture dripped from the same ledge in the wall on to the sodden leaves beneath, as it had done all through the afternoons of all those past Novembers. This was the place, this damp and gloomy tangle, that had specially belonged to me. Nobody ever came to it, for in winter it was too dreary, and in summer so full of mosquitoes that only a Backfisch indifferent to spots could have borne it. But it was a place where I could play unobserved, and where I could walk up and down uninterrupted for hours, building castles in the air. There was an unwholesome little arbour in one dark corner, much frequented by the larger black slug, where I used to pass glorious afternoons making plans. I was for ever making plans, and if nothing came of them, what did it matter? The mere making had been a joy. To me this out-of-the-way corner was always a wonderful and a mysterious place, where my castles in the air stood close together in radiant rows, and where the strangest and most splendid adventures befell me; for the hours I passed in it and the people I met in it were all enchanted.

Standing there and looking round with happy eyes, I forgot the existence of the cousins. I could have cried for joy at being there again. It was the home of my fathers, the home that would have been mine if I had been a boy, the home that was mine now by a thousand tender and happy and miserable associations, of which the people in possession could not dream. They were tenants, but it was my home. I threw my arms round the trunk of a very wet fir tree, every branch of which I remembered, for had I not climbed it, and fallen from it, and torn and bruised myself on it uncountable numbers of times? and I gave it such a hearty kiss that my nose and chin were smudged into one green stain, and still I did not care. Far from caring, it filled me with a reckless, Backfisch pleasure in being dirty, a delicious feeling that I had not had for years. Alice in Wonderland, after she had drunk the contents of the magic bottle, could not have grown smaller more suddenly than I grew younger the moment I passed through that magic door. Bad habits cling to us, however, with such persistency that I did mechanically pull out my handkerchief and begin to rub off the welcoming smudge, a thing I never would have dreamed of doing in the glorious old days; but an artful scent of violets clinging to the handkerchief brought me to my senses, and with a sudden impulse of scorn, the fine scorn for scent of every honest Backfisch, I rolled it up into a ball and flung it away into the bushes, where I daresay it is at this moment. 'Away with you,' I cried, 'away with you, symbol of conventionality, of slavery, of pandering to a desire to please — away with you, miserable little lace-edged rag!' And so young had I grown within the last few minutes that I did not even feel silly.

As a Backfisch I had never used handkerchiefs — the child of nature scorns to blow its nose — though for decency's sake my governess insisted on giving me a clean one of vast size and stubborn texture on Sundays. It was stowed away unfolded in the remotest corner of my pocket, where it was gradually pressed into a beautiful compactness by the other contents, which were knives. After a while, I remember, the handkerchief being brought to light on Sundays to make room for a successor, and being manifestly perfectly clean, we came to an agreement that it should only be changed on the first and third Sundays in the month, on condition that I promised to turn it on the other Sundays. My governess said that the outer folds became soiled from the mere contact with the other things in my pocket, and that visitors might catch sight of the soiled side if it was never turned when I wished to blow my nose in their presence, and that one had no right to give one's visitors shocks. 'But I never do wish — ' I began with great earnestness. 'Unsinn,' said my governess, cutting me short.

After the first thrills of joy at being there again had gone, the profound stillness of the dripping little shrubbery frightened me. It was so still that I was afraid to move; so still, that I could count each drop of moisture falling from the oozing wall; so still, that when I held my breath to listen, I was deafened by my own heart-beats. I made a step forward in the direction where the arbour ought to be, and the rustling and jingling of my clothes terrified me into immobility. The house was only two hundred yards off; and if any one had been about, the noise I had already made opening the creaking door and so foolishly apostrophising my handkerchief must have been noticed. Suppose an inquiring gardener, or a restless cousin, should presently loom through the fog, bearing down upon me? Suppose Fräulein Wundermacher should pounce upon me suddenly from behind, coming up noiselessly in her galoshes, and shatter my castles with her customary triumphant 'Fetzt halte ich dich aber fest!' Why, what was I thinking of? Fräulein Wundermacher, so big and masterful, such an enemy of day-dreams, such a friend of das Praktische, such a lover of creature comforts, had died long ago, had been succeeded long ago by others, German sometimes, and sometimes English, and sometimes at intervals French, and they too had all in their turn vanished, and I was here a solitary ghost. 'Come, Elizabeth,' said I to myself impatiently, 'are you actually growing sentimental over your governesses? If you think you are a ghost, be glad at least that you are a solitary one. Would you like the ghosts of all those poor women you tormented to rise up now in this gloomy place against you?

And do you intend to stand here till you are caught?' And thus exhorting myself to action, and recognising how great was the risk I ran in lingering, I started down the little path leading to the arbour and the principal part of the garden, going, it is true, on tiptoe, and very much frightened by the rustling of my petticoats, but determined to see what I had come to see and not to be scared away by phantoms.

How regretfully did I think at that moment of the petticoats of my youth, so short, so silent, and so woollen! And how convenient the canvas shoes were with the india rubber soles, for creeping about without making a sound! Thanks to them I could always run swiftly and unheard into my hiding-places, and stay there listening to the garden resounding with cries of 'Elizabeth! Elizabeth! Come in at once to your lessons!' Or, at a different period, 'Ou êtes-vous donc, petite sotte?' Or at yet another period, 'Warte nur, wenn ich dich erst habe!' As the voices came round one corner, I whisked in my noiseless clothes round the next, and it was only Fräulein Wundermacher, a person of resource, who discovered that all she needed for my successful circumvention was galoshes. She purchased a pair, wasted no breath calling me, and would come up silently, as I stood lapped in a false security lost in the contemplation of a squirrel or a robin, and seize me by the shoulders from behind, to the grievous unhinging of my nerves. Stealing along in the fog, I looked back uneasily once or twice, so vivid was this disquieting memory, and could hardly be reassured by putting up my hand to the elaborate twists and curls that compose what my maid calls my Frisur, and that mark the gulf lying between the present and the past; for it had happened once or twice, awful to relate and to remember, that Fräulein Wundermacher, sooner than let me slip through her fingers, had actually caught me by the long plait of hair to whose other end I was attached and whose English name I had been told was pigtail, just at the instant when I was springing away from her into the bushes; and so had led me home triumphant, holding on tight to the rope of hair, and muttering with a broad smile of special satisfaction, 'Diesmal wirst du mir aber nicht entschlupfen!' Fräulein Wundermacher, now I came to think of it, must have been a humourist. She was certainly a clever and a capable woman. But I wished at that moment that she would not haunt me so persistently, and that I could get rid of the feeling that she was just behind in her galoshes, with her hand stretched out to seize me. Passing the arbour, and peering into its damp recesses, I started back with my heart in my mouth. I thought I saw my grandfather's stern eyes shining in the darkness. It was evident that my anxiety lest the cousins should catch me had quite upset my nerves, for I am not by nature inclined to see eyes where eyes are not. 'Don't be foolish, Elizabeth,' murmured my soul in rather a faint voice, 'go in, and make sure.' 'But I don't like going in and making sure,' I replied. I did go in, however, with a sufficient show of courage, and fortunately the eyes vanished. What I should have done if they had not I am altogether unable to imagine. Ghosts are things that I laugh at in the daytime and fear at night, but I think if I were to meet one I should die. The arbour had fallen into great decay, and was in the last stage of mouldiness. My grandfather had had it made, and, like other buildings, it enjoyed a period of prosperity before being left to the ravages of slugs and children, when he came down every afternoon in summer and drank his coffee there and read his Kreuzzeitung and dozed, while the rest of us went about on tiptoe, and only the birds dared sing. Even the mosquitoes that infested the place were too much in awe of him to sting him; they certainly never did sting him, and I naturally concluded it must be because he had forbidden such familiarities. Although I had played there for so many years since his death, my memory skipped them all, and went back to the days when it was exclusively his. Standing on the spot where his armchair used to be, I felt how well I knew him now from the impressions he made then on my child's mind, though I was not conscious of them for more than twenty years. Nobody told me about him, and he died when I was six, and yet within the last year or two, that strange Indian summer of remembrance that comes to us in the leisured times when the children have been born and we have time to think, has made me know him perfectly well. It is rather an uncomfortable thought for the grown-up, and especially for the parent, but of a salutary and restraining nature, that though children may not understand what is said and done before them, and have no interest in it at the time, and though they may forget it at once and for years, yet these things that they have seen and heard and not noticed have after all impressed themselves for ever on their minds, and when they are men and women come crowding back with surprising and often painful distinctness, and away frisk all the cherished little illusions in flocks.

I had an awful reverence for my grandfather. He never petted, and he often frowned, and such people are generally reverenced. Besides, he was a just man, everybody said; a just man who might have been a great man if he had chosen, and risen to almost any pinnacle of worldly glory. That he had not so chosen was held to be a convincing proof of his greatness; for he was plainly too great to be great in the vulgar sense, and shrouded himself in the dignity of privacy and potentialities. This, at least, as time passed and he still did nothing, was the belief of the simple people around. People must believe in somebody, and having pinned their faith on my grandfather in the promising years that lie round thirty, it was more convenient to let it remain there. He pervaded our family life till my sixth year, and saw to it that we all behaved ourselves, and then he died, and we were glad that he should be in heaven. He was a good German (and when Germans are good they are very good) who kept the commandments, voted for the Government, grew prize potatoes and bred innumerable sheep, drove to Berlin once a year with the wool in a procession of waggons behind him and sold it at the annual Woll-markt, rioted soberly for a few days there, and then carried most of the proceeds home, hunted as often as possible, helped his friends, punished his children, read his Bible, said his prayers, and was genuinely astonished when his wife had the affectation to die of a broken heart. I cannot pretend to explain this conduct. She ought, of course, to have been happy in the possession of so good a man; but good men are sometimes oppressive, and to have one in the house with you and to live in the daily glare of his goodness must be a tremendous business. After bearing him seven sons and three daughters, therefore, my grandmother died in the way described, and afforded, said my grandfather, another and a very curious proof of the impossibility of ever being sure of your ground with women. The incident faded more quickly from his mind than it might otherwise have done for its having occurred simultaneously with the production of a new kind of potato, of which he was justly proud. He called it Trost in Trauer, and quoted the text of Scripture Auge um Auge, Zahn um Zahn, after which he did not again allude to his wife's decease. In his last years, when my father managed the estate, and he only lived with us and criticised, he came to have the reputation of an oracle. The neighbours sent him their sons at the beginning of any important phase in their lives, and he received them in this very arbour, administering eloquent and minute advice in the deep voice that rolled round the shrubbery and filled me with a vague sense of guilt as I played. Sitting among the bushes playing muffled games for fear of disturbing him, I supposed he must be reading aloud, so unbroken was the monotony of that majestic roll. The young men used to come out again bathed in perspiration, much stung by mosquitoes, and looking bewildered; and when they had got over the impression made by my grandfather's speech and presence, no doubt forgot all he had said with wholesome quickness, and set themselves to the interesting and necessary work of gaining their own experience. Once, indeed, a dreadful thing happened, whose immediate consequence was the abrupt end to the long and close friendship between us and our nearest neighbour. His son was brought to the arbour and left there in the usual way, and either he must have happened on the critical half hour after the coffee and before the Kreuzzeitung, when my grandfather was accustomed to sleep, or he was more courageous than the others and tried to talk, for very shortly, playing as usual near at hand, I heard my grandfather's voice, raised to an extent that made me stop in my game and quake, saying with deliberate anger, 'Hebe dich weg von mir, Sohn des Satans!' Which was all the advice this particular young man got, and which he hastened to take, for out he came through the bushes, and though his face was very pale, there was an odd twist about the corners of his mouth that reassured me.

This must have happened quite at the end of my grandfather's life, for almost immediately afterwards, as it now seems to me, he died before he need have done because he would eat crab, a dish that never agreed with him, in the face of his doctor's warning that if he did he would surely die. 'What! am I to be conquered by crabs?' he demanded indignantly of the doctor; for apart from loving them with all his heart he had never yet been conquered by anything. 'Nay, sir, the combat is too unequal — do not, I pray you, try it again,' replied the doctor. But my grandfather ordered crabs that very night for supper, and went in to table with the shining eyes of one who is determined to conquer or die, and the crabs conquered, and he died. 'He was a just man,' said the neighbours, except that nearest neighbour, formerly his best friend, 'and might have been a great one had he so chosen.' And they buried him with profound respect, and the sunshine came into our home life with a burst, and the birds were not the only creatures that sang, and the arbour, from having been a temple of Delphic utterances, sank into a home for slugs.

Musing on the strangeness of life, and on the invariable ultimate triumph of the insignificant and small over the important and vast, illustrated in this instance by the easy substitution in the arbour of slugs for grandfathers, I went slowly round the next bend of the path, and came to the broad walk along the south side of the high wall dividing the flower garden from the kitchen garden, in which sheltered position my father had had his choicest flowers. Here the cousins had been at work, and all the climbing roses that clothed the wall with beauty were gone, and some very neat fruit trees, tidily nailed up at proper intervals, reigned in their stead. Evidently the cousins knew the value of this warm aspect, for in the border beneath, filled in my father's time in this month of November with the wallflowers that were to perfume the walk in spring, there was a thick crop of — I stooped down close to make sure — yes, a thick crop of radishes. My eyes filled with tears at the sight of those radishes, and it is probably the only occasion on record on which radishes have made anybody cry. My dear father, whom I so passionately loved, had in his turn passionately loved this particular border, and spent the spare moments of a busy life enjoying the flowers that grew in it. He had no time himself for a more near acquaintance with the delights of gardening than directing what plants were to be used, but found rest from his daily work strolling up and down here, or sitting smoking as close to the flowers as possible. 'It is the Purest of Humane pleasures, it is the Greatest Refreshment to the Spirits of Man,' he would quote (for he read other things besides the Kreuzzeitung), looking round with satisfaction on reaching this fragrant haven after a hot day in the fields. Well, the cousins did not think so. Less fanciful, and more sensible as they probably would have said, their position plainly was that you cannot eat flowers. Their spirits required no refreshment, but their bodies needed much, and therefore radishes were more precious than wallflowers. Nor was my youth wholly destitute of radishes, but they were grown in the decent obscurity of odd kitchen garden corners and old cucumber frames, and would never have been allowed to come among the flowers. And only because I was not a boy here they were profaning the ground that used to be so beautiful. Oh, it was a terrible misfortune not to have been a boy! And how sad and lonely it was, after all, in this ghostly garden. The radish bed and what it symbolised had turned my first joy into grief. This walk and border me too much of my father reminded, and of all he had been to me. What I knew of good he had taught me, and what I had of happiness was through him. Only once during all the years we lived together had we been of different opinions and fallen out, and it was the one time I ever saw him severe. I was four years old, and demanded one Sunday to be taken to church. My father said no, for I had never been to church, and the German service is long and exhausting. I implored. He again said no. I implored again, and showed such a pious disposition, and so earnest a determination to behave well, that he gave in, and we went off very happily hand in hand. 'Now mind, Elizabeth,' he said, turning to me at the church door, 'there is no coming out again in the middle. Having insisted on being brought, thou shalt now sit patiently till the end.' 'Oh, yes, oh, yes,' I promised eagerly, and went in filled with holy fire. The shortness of my legs, hanging helplessly for two hours midway between the seat and the floor, was the weapon chosen by Satan for my destruction. In German churches you do not kneel, and seldom stand, but sit nearly the whole time, praying and singing in great comfort. If you are four years old, however, this unchanged position soon becomes one of torture. Unknown and dreadful things go on in your legs, strange prickings and tinglings and dartings up and down, a sudden terrifying numbness, when you think they must have dropped off but are afraid to look, then renewed and fiercer prickings, shootings, and burnings. I thought I must be very ill, for I had never known my legs like that before. My father sitting beside me was engrossed in the singing of a chorale that evidently had no end, each verse finished with a long-drawn-out hallelujah, after which the organ played by itself for a hundred years — by the organist's watch, which was wrong, two minutes exactly — and then another verse began. My father, being the patron of the living, was careful to sing and pray and listen to the sermon with exemplary attention, aware that every eye in the little church was on our pew, and at first I tried to imitate him; but the behaviour of my legs became so alarming that after vainly casting imploring glances at him and seeing that he continued his singing unmoved, I put out my hand and pulled his sleeve.

'Hal-le-lu-jah,' sang my father with deliberation; continuing in a low voice without changing the expression of his face, his lips hardly moving, and his eyes fixed abstractedly on the ceiling till the organist, who was also the postman, should have finished his solo, 'Did I not tell thee to sit still, Elizabeth?' 'Yes, but — ' 'Then do it.' 'But I want to go home.'

'Unsinn.' And the next verse beginning, my

father sang louder than ever. What could I do? Should I cry? I began to be afraid I was going to die on that chair, so extraordinary were the sensations in my legs. What could my father do to me if I did cry? With the quick instinct of small children I felt that he could not put me in the corner in church, nor would he whip me in public, and that with the whole village looking on, he was helpless, and would have to give in. Therefore I tugged his sleeve again and more peremptorily, and prepared to demand my immediate removal in a loud voice. But my father was ready for me. Without interrupting his singing, or altering his devout expression, he put his hand slowly down and gave me a hard pinch — not a playful pinch, but a good hard unmistakeable pinch, such as I had never imagined possible, and then went on serenely to the next hallelujah. For a moment I was petrified with astonishment. Was this my indulgent father, my playmate, adorer, and friend? Smarting with pain, for I was a round baby, with a nicely stretched, tight skin, and dreadfully hurt in my feelings, I opened my mouth to shriek in earnest, when my father's clear whisper fell on my ear, each word distinct and not to be misunderstood, his eyes as before gazing meditatively into space, and his lips hardly moving, 'Elizabeth, wenn du schreist, kneife ich dich bis du platzt.' And he finished the verse with unruffled decorum —

> 'Will Satan mich verschlingen,
> So lass die Engel singen
> Hallelujah!'

We never had another difference. Up to then he had been my willing slave, and after that I was his.

With a smile and a shiver I turned from the border and its memories to the door in the wall leading to the kitchen garden, in a corner of which my own little garden used to be. The door was open, and I stood still a moment before going through, to hold my breath and listen. The silence was as profound as before. The place seemed deserted; and I should have thought the house empty and shut up but for the carefully tended radishes and the recent footmarks on the green of the path. They were the footmarks of a child. I was stooping down to examine a specially clear one, when the loud caw of a very bored looking crow sitting on the wall just above my head made me jump as I have seldom in my life jumped, and reminded me that I was trespassing. Clearly my nerves were all to pieces, for I gathered up my skirts and fled through the door as though a whole army of ghosts and cousins were at my heels, nor did I stop till I had reached the remote corner where my garden was. 'Are you enjoying yourself, Elizabeth?' asked the mocking sprite that calls itself my soul: but I was too much out of breath to answer.

This was really a very safe corner. It was separated from the main garden and the house by the wall, and shut in on the north side by an orchard, and it was to the last degree unlikely that any one would come there on such an afternoon. This plot of ground, turned now as I saw into a rockery, had been the scene of my most untiring labours. Into the cold earth of this north border on which the sun never shone I had dug my brightest hopes. All my pocket money had been spent on it, and as bulbs were dear and my weekly allowance small, in a fatal hour I had borrowed from Fräulein Wunder-macher, selling her my independence, passing utterly into her power, forced as a result till my next birthday should come round to an unnatural suavity of speech and manner in her company, against which my very soul revolted. And after all, nothing came up. The labour of digging and watering, the anxious zeal with which I pounced on weeds, the poring over gardening books, the plans made as I sat on the little seat in the middle gazing admiringly and with the eye of faith on the trim surface so soon to be gemmed with a thousand flowers, the reckless expenditure of pfennigs, the humiliation of my position in regard to Fräulein Wundermacher, — all, all had been in vain. No sun shone there, and nothing grew. The gardener who reigned supreme in those days had given me this big piece for that sole reason, because he could do nothing with it himself. He was no doubt of opinion that it was quite good enough for a child to experiment upon, and went his way, when I had thanked him with a profuseness of gratitude I still remember, with an unmoved countenance. For more than a year I worked and waited, and watched the career of the flourishing orchard opposite with puzzled feelings. The orchard was only a few yards away, and yet, although my garden was full of manure, and water, and attentions that were never bestowed on the orchard, all it could show and ever did show were a few unhappy beginnings of growth that either remained stationary and did not achieve flowers, or dwindled down again and vanished. Once I timidly asked the gardener if he could explain these signs and wonders, but he was a busy man with no time for answering questions, and told me shortly that gardening was not learned in a day. How well

I remember that afternoon, and the very shape of the lazy clouds, and the smell of spring things, and myself going away abashed and sitting on the shaky bench in my domain and wondering for the hundredth time what it was that made the difference between my bit and the bit of orchard in front of me. The fruit trees, far enough away from the wall to be beyond the reach of its cold shade, were tossing their flower-laden heads in the sunshine in a carelessly well-satisfied fashion that filled my heart with envy. There was a rise in the field behind them, and at the foot of its protecting slope they luxuriated in the insolent glory of their white and pink perfection. It was May, and my heart bled at the thought of the tulips I had put in in November, and that I had never seen since. The whole of the rest of the garden was on fire with tulips; behind me, on the other side of the wall, were rows and rows of them, — cups of translucent loveliness, a jewelled ring flung right round the lawn. But what was there not on the other side of that wall? Things came up there and grew and flowered exactly as my gardening books said they should do; and in front of me, in the gay orchard, things that nobody ever troubled about or cultivated or noticed throve joyously beneath the trees, — daffodils thrusting their spears through the grass, crocuses peeping out inquiringly, snowdrops uncovering their small cold faces when the first shivering spring days came. Only my piece that I so loved was perpetually ugly and empty. And I sat in it thinking of these things on that radiant day, and wept aloud.

Then an apprentice came by, a youth who had often seen me busily digging, and noticing the unusual tears, and struck perhaps by the difference between my garden and the profusion of splendour all around, paused with his barrow on the path in front of me, and remarked that nobody could expect to get blood out of a stone. The apparent irrelevance of this statement made me weep still louder, the bitter tears of insulted sorrow; but he stuck to his point, and harangued me from the path, explaining the connection between north walls and tulips and blood and stones till my tears all dried up again and I listened attentively, for the conclusion to be drawn from his remarks was plainly that I had been shamefully taken in by the head gardener, who was an unprincipled person thenceforward to be for ever mistrusted and shunned. Standing on the path from which the kindly apprentice had expounded his proverb, this scene rose before me as clearly as though it had taken place that very day; but how different everything looked, and how it had shrunk! Was this the wide orchard that had seemed to stretch away, it and the sloping field beyond, up to the gates of heaven? I believe nearly every child who is much alone goes through a certain time of hourly expecting the Day of Judgment, and I had made up my mind that on that Day the heavenly host would enter the world by that very field, coming down the slope in shining ranks, treading the daffodils under foot, filling the orchard with their songs of exultation, joyously seeking out the sheep from among the goats. Of course I was a sheep, and my governess and the head gardener goats, so that the results could not fail to be in every way satisfactory. But looking up at the slope and remembering my visions, I laughed at the smallness of the field I had supposed would hold all heaven.

Here again the cousins had been at work. The site of my garden was occupied by a rockery, and the orchard grass with all its treasures had been dug up, and the spaces between the trees planted with currant bushes and celery in admirable rows; so that no future little cousins will be able to dream of celestial hosts coming towards them across the fields of daffodils, and will perhaps be the better for being free from visions of the kind, for as I grew older, uncomfortable doubts laid hold of my heart with cold fingers, dim uncertainties as to the exact ultimate position of the gardener and the governess, anxious questionings as to how it would be if it were they who turned out after all to be sheep, and I who — ? For that we all three might be gathered into the same fold at the last never, in those days, struck me as possible, and if it had I should not have liked it.

'Now what sort of person can that be,' I asked myself, shaking my head, as I contemplated the changes before me, 'who could put a rockery among vegetables and currant bushes? A rockery, of all things in the gardening world, needs consummate tact in its treatment. It is easier to make mistakes in forming a rockery than in any other garden scheme. Either it is a great success, or it is great failure; either it is very charming, or it is very absurd. There is no state between the sublime and the ridiculous possible in a rockery.' I stood shaking my head disapprovingly at the rockery before me, lost in these reflections, when a sudden quick pattering of feet coming along in a great hurry made me turn round with a start, just in time to receive the shock of a body tumbling out of the mist and knocking violently against me.

It was a little girl of about twelve years old.

'Hullo!' said the little girl in excellent English; and then we stared at each other in astonishment.

'I thought you were Miss Robinson,' said the little girl, offering no apology for having nearly knocked me down. 'Who are you?'

'Miss Robinson? Miss Robinson?' I repeated, my eyes fixed on the little girl's face, and a host of memories stirring within me. 'Why, didn't she marry a missionary, and go out to some place where they ate him?'

The little girl stared harder. 'Ate him? Marry? What, has she been married all this time to somebody who's been eaten and never let on? Oh, I say, what a game!' And she threw back her head and laughed till the garden rang again.

'O hush, you dreadful little girl!' I implored, catching her by the arm, and terrified beyond measure by the loudness of her mirth. 'Don't make that horrid noise — we are certain to be caught if you don't stop — '

The little girl broke off a shriek of laughter in the middle and shut her mouth with a snap. Her eyes, round and black and shiny like boot buttons, came still further out of her head. 'Caught?' she said eagerly. 'What, are you afraid of being caught too? Well, this is a game!' And with her hands plunged deep in the pockets of her coat she capered in front of me in the excess of her enjoyment, reminding me of a very fat black lamb frisking round the dazed and passive sheep its mother.

It was clear that the time had come for me to get down to the gate at the end of the garden as quickly as possible, and I began to move away in that direction. The little girl at once stopped capering and planted herself squarely in front of me. 'Who are you?' she said, examining me from my hat to my boots with the keenest interest.

I considered this ungarnished manner of asking questions impertinent, and, trying to look lofty, made an attempt to pass at the side.

The little girl, with a quick, cork-like movement, was there before me.

'Who are you?' she repeated, her expression friendly but firm. 'Oh, I — I'm a pilgrim,' I said in desperation.

'A pilgrim!' echoed the little girl. She seemed struck, and while she was struck I slipped past her and began to walk quickly towards the door in the wall. 'A pilgrim!' said the little girl, again, keeping close beside me, and looking me up and down attentively. 'I don't like pilgrims. Aren't they people who are always walking about, and have things the matter with their feet? Have you got anything the matter with your feet?'

'Certainly not,' I replied indignantly, walking still faster. 'And they never wash, Miss Robinson says. You don't either, do you?'

'Not wash? Oh, I'm afraid you are a very badly brought-up little girl — oh, leave me alone — I must run — '

'So must I,' said the little girl, cheerfully, 'for Miss Robinson must be close behind us. She nearly had me just before I found you.' And she started running by my side.

The thought of Miss Robinson close behind us gave wings to my feet, and, casting my dignity, of which, indeed, there was but little left, to the winds, I fairly flew down the path. The little girl was not to be outrun, and though she panted and turned weird colours, kept by my side and even talked. Oh, I was tired, tired in body and mind, tired by the different shocks I had received, tired by the journey, tired by the want of food; and here I was being forced to run because this very naughty little girl chose to hide instead of going in to her lessons.

'I say — this is jolly — ' she jerked out.

'But why need we run to the same place?' I breathlessly asked, in the vain hope of getting rid of her. 'Oh, yes — that's just — the fun. We'd get on — together — you and I — '

'No, no,' said I, decided on this point,

bewildered though I was.

'I can't stand washing — either — it's awful — in winter — and makes one have — chaps.'

'But I don't mind it in the least,' I protested faintly, not having any energy left.

'Oh, I say!' said the little girl, looking at my face, and making the sound known as a guffaw. The familiarity of this little girl was wholly revolting.

We had got safely through the door, round the corner past the radishes, and were in the shrubbery. I knew from experience how easy it was to hide in the tangle of little paths, and stopped a moment to look round and listen. The little girl opened her mouth to speak. With great presence of mind I instantly put my muff in front of it and held it there tight, while I listened. Dead silence, except for the laboured breathing and struggles of the little girl.

'I don't hear a sound,' I whispered, letting her go again. 'Now what did you want to say?' I added, eyeing her severely.

'I wanted to say,' she panted, 'that it's no good pretending you wash with a nose like that.'

'A nose like that! A nose like what?' I exclaimed, greatly offended; and though I put up my hand and very tenderly and carefully felt it, I could find no difference in it. 'I am afraid poor Miss Robinson must have a wretched life,' I said, in tones of deep disgust.

The little girl smiled fatuously, as though I were paying her compliments. 'It's all green and brown,' she said, pointing. 'Is it always like that?'

Then I remembered the wet fir tree near the gate, and the enraptured kiss it had received, and blushed.

'Won't it come off?' persisted the little girl.

'Of course it will come off,' I answered, frowning.

'Why don't you rub it off?'

Then I remembered the throwing away of the handkerchief, and blushed again.

'Please lend me your handkerchief,' I said humbly, 'I — I have lost mine.'

There was a great fumbling in six different pockets, and then a handkerchief that made me young again merely to look at it was produced. I took it thankfully and rubbed with energy, the little girl, intensely inter-ested, watching the operation and giving me advice. 'There — it's all right now — a little more on the right — there — now it's all off.'

'Are you sure? No green left?' I anxiously asked.

'No, it's red all over now,' she replied cheerfully. 'Let me get home,' thought I, very much upset by this information, 'let me get home to my dear, uncritical, admiring babies, who accept my nose as an example of what a nose should be, and whatever its colour think it beautiful.' And thrusting the handkerchief back into the little girl's hands, I hurried away down the path. She packed it away hastily, but it took some seconds for it was of the size of a small sheet, and then came running after me. 'Where are you going?' she asked surprised, as I turned down the path leading to the gate.

'Through this gate,' I replied with decision.

'But you mustn't — we're not allowed to go through there — '

So strong was the force of old habits in that place that at the words not allowed my hand dropped of itself from the latch; and at that instant a voice calling quite close to us through the mist struck me rigid.

'Elizabeth! Elizabeth!' called the voice, 'Come in at once to your lessons — Elizabeth! Elizabeth!'

'It's Miss Robinson,' whispered the little girl, twinkling with excitement; then, catching sight of my face, she said once more with eager insistence, 'Who are you?'

'Oh, I'm a ghost!' I cried with conviction, pressing my hands to my forehead and looking round fearfully.

'Pooh,' said the little girl.

It was the last remark I heard her make, for there was a creaking of approaching boots in the bushes, and seized by a frightful panic I pulled the gate open with one desperate pull, flung it to behind me, and fled out and away down the wide, misty fields.

The Gotha Almanach says that the reigning cousin married the daughter of a Mr. Johnstone, an Englishman, in 1885, and that in 1886 their only child was born, Elizabeth.

⋆ ⋆ ⋆

November 20th. — Last night we had ten degrees of frost (Fahrenheit), and I went out the first thing this morning to see what had become of the tea-roses, and behold, they were wide awake and quite cheerful — covered with rime it is true, but anything but black and shrivelled. Even those in boxes on each side of the verandah steps were perfectly alive and full of buds, and one in particular, a Bouquet d'Or, is a mass of buds, and would flower if it could get the least encouragement. I am beginning to think that the tenderness of tea-roses is much exaggerated, and am certainly very glad I had the courage to try them in this northern garden. But I must not fly too boldly in the face of Providence, and have ordered those in the boxes to be taken into the greenhouse for the winter, and hope the Bouquet d'Or, in a sunny place near the glass, may be induced to open some of those buds. The greenhouse is only used as a refuge, and kept at a temperature just above freezing, and is reserved entirely for such plants as cannot stand the very coldest part of the winter out of doors. I don't use it for growing anything, because I don't love things that will only bear the garden for three or four months in the year and require coaxing and petting for the rest of it. Give me a garden full of strong, healthy creatures, able to stand roughness and cold without dismally giving in and dying. I never could see that delicacy of constitution is pretty, either in plants or women. No doubt there are many lovely flowers to be had by heat and constant coaxing, but then for each of these there are fifty others still lovelier that will gratefully grow in God's wholesome air and are blessed in return with a far greater intensity of scent and colour.

We have been very busy till now getting the permanent beds into order and planting the new tea-roses, and I am looking forward to next summer with more hope than ever in spite of my many failures. I wish the years would pass quickly that will bring my garden to perfection! The Persian Yellows have gone into their new quarters, and their place is occupied by the tea-rose Safrano; all the rose beds are carpeted with pansies sown in July and transplanted in October, each bed having a separate colour. The purple ones are the most charming and go well with every rose, but I have white ones with Laurette Messimy, and yellow ones with Safrano, and a new red sort in the big centre bed of red roses. Round the semicircle on the south side of the little privet hedge two rows of annual larkspurs in all their delicate shades have been sown, and just beyond the larkspurs, on the grass, is a semicircle of standard tea and pillar roses.

In front of the house the long borders have been stocked with larkspurs, annual and perennial, columbines, giant poppies, pinks, Madonna lilies, wallflowers, hollyhocks, perennial phloxes, peonies, lavender, starworts, cornflowers, Lychnis chalcedonica, and bulbs packed in wherever bulbs could go. These are the borders that were so hardly used by the other gardener. The spring boxes for the verandah steps have been filled with pink and white and yellow tulips. I love tulips better than any other spring flower; they are the embodiment of alert cheerfulness and tidy grace, and next to a hyacinth look like a wholesome, freshly tubbed young girl beside a stout lady whose every movement weighs down the air with patchouli. Their faint, delicate scent is refinement itself; and is there anything in the world more charming than the sprightly way they hold up their little faces to the sun. I have heard them called bold and flaunting, but to me they seem modest grace itself, only always on the alert to enjoy life as much as they can and not afraid of looking the sun or anything else above them in the face. On the grass there are two beds of them carpeted with forget-me-nots; and in the grass, in scattered groups, are daffodils and narcissus. Down the wilder shrubbery walks foxgloves and mulleins will (I hope) shine majestic; and one cool corner, backed by a group of firs, is graced by Madonna lilies, white foxgloves, and columbines.

In a distant glade I have made a spring garden round an oak tree that stands alone in the sun — groups of crocuses, daffodils, narcissus, hyacinths, and tulips, among such flowering shrubs and trees as Pirus Malus spectabilis, floribunda, and coronaria; Prunus Juliana, Mahaleb, serotina, triloba, and Pissardi; Cydonias and Weigelias in every colour, and several kinds of Crataegus and other May lovelinesses. If the weather behaves itself nicely, and we get gentle rains in due season, I think this little corner will be beautiful — but what a big 'if' it is! Drought is our great enemy, and the two last summers each contained five weeks of blazing, cloudless heat when all the ditches dried up and the soil was like hot pastry. At such times the watering is naturally quite beyond the strength of two men; but as a garden is a place to be happy in, and not one where you want to meet a dozen curious eyes at every turn, I should not like to have more than these two, or rather one and a half — the assistant having stork-like proclivities and going home in the autumn to his native Russia, returning in the spring with the first warm winds. I want to keep him over the winter, as there is much to be done even then, and I sounded him on the point the other day. He is the most abject-looking of human beings — lame, and afflicted with a hideous eye-disease; but he is a good worker and plods along unwearyingly from sunrise to dusk.

'Pray, my good stork,' said I, or German words to that effect, 'why don't you stay here altogether, instead of going home and rioting away all you have earned?'

'I would stay,' he answered, 'but I have my wife there in Russia.'

'Your wife!' I exclaimed, stupidly surprised that the poor deformed creature should have found a mate — as though there were not a superfluity of mates in the world — 'I didn't know you were married?'

'Yes, and I have two little children, and I don't know what they would do if I were not to come home. But it is a very expensive journey to Russia, and costs me every time seven marks.'

'Seven marks!'

'Yes, it is a great sum.'

I wondered whether I should be able to get to Russia for seven marks, supposing I were to be seized with an unnatural craving to go there.

All the labourers who work here from March to December are Russians and Poles, or a mixture of both. We send a man over who can speak their language, to fetch as many as he can early in the year, and they arrive with their bundles, men and women and babies, and as soon as they have got here and had their fares paid, they disappear in the night if they get the chance, sometimes fifty of them at a time, to go and work singly or in couples for the peasants, who pay them a pfennig or two more a day than we do, and let them eat with the family. From us they get a mark and a half to two marks a day, and as many potatoes as they can eat. The women get less, not because they work less, but because they are women and must not be encouraged. The overseer lives with them, and has a loaded revolver in his pocket and a savage dog at his heels. For the first week or two after their arrival, the foresters and other permanent officials keep guard at night over the houses they are put into. I suppose they find it sleepy work; for certain it is that spring after spring the same thing happens, fifty of them getting away in spite of all our precautions, and we are left with our mouths open and much out of pocket. This spring, by some mistake, they arrived without their bundles, which had gone astray on the road, and, as they travel in their best clothes, they refused utterly to work until their luggage came. Nearly a week was lost waiting, to the despair of all in authority.

Nor will any persuasions induce them to do anything on Saints' days, and there surely never was a church so full of them as the Russian Church. In the spring, when every hour is of vital importance, the work is constantly being interrupted by them, and the workers lie sleeping in the sun the whole day, agreeably conscious that they are pleasing themselves and the Church at one and the same time — a state of perfection as rare as it is desirable. Reason unaided by Faith is of course exasperated at this waste of precious time, and I confess that during the first mild days after the long winter frost when it is possible to begin to work the ground, I have sympathised with the gloom of the Man of Wrath, confronted in one week by two or three empty days on which no man will labour, and have listened in silence to his remarks about distant Russian saints.

I suppose it was my own superfluous amount of civilisation that made me pity these people when first I came to live among them. They herd together like animals and do the work of animals; but in spite of the armed overseer, the dirt and the rags, the meals of potatoes washed down by weak vinegar and water, I am beginning to believe that they would strongly object to soap, I am sure they would not wear new clothes, and I hear them coming home from their work at dusk singing. They are like little children or animals in their utter inability to grasp the idea of a future; and after all, if you work all day in God's sunshine, when evening comes you are pleasantly tired and ready for rest and not much inclined to find fault with your lot. I have not yet persuaded myself, however, that the women are happy. They have to work as hard as the men and get less for it; they have to produce offspring, quite regardless of times and seasons and the general fitness of things; they have to do this as expeditiously as possible, so that they may not unduly interrupt the work in hand; nobody helps them, notices them, or cares about them, least of all the husband. It is quite a usual thing to see them working in the fields in the morning, and working again in the afternoon, having in the interval produced a baby. The baby is left to an old woman whose duty it is to look after babies collectively. When I expressed my horror at the poor creatures working immediately afterwards as though nothing had happened, the Man of Wrath informed me that they did not suffer because they had never worn corsets, nor had their mothers and grandmothers. We were riding together at the time, and had just passed a batch of workers, and my husband was speaking to the overseer, when a woman arrived alone, and taking up a spade, began to dig. She grinned cheerfully at us as she made a curtesy, and the overseer remarked that she had just been back to the house and had a baby.

'Poor, poor woman!' I cried, as we rode on, feeling for some occult reason very angry with the Man of Wrath. 'And her wretched husband doesn't care a rap, and will probably beat her to-night if his supper isn't right. What nonsense it is to talk about the equality of the sexes when the women have the babies!'

'Quite so, my dear,' replied the Man of Wrath, smiling condescendingly. 'You have got to the very root of the matter. Nature, while imposing this agreeable duty on the woman, weakens her and disables her for any serious competition with man. How can a person who is constantly losing a year of the best part of her life compete with a young man who never loses any time at all? He has the brute force, and his last word on any subject could always be his fist.'

I said nothing. It was a dull, gray afternoon in the beginning of November, and the leaves dropped slowly and silently at our horses' feet as we rode towards the Hirschwald.

'It is a universal custom,' proceeded the Man of Wrath, 'amongst these Russians, and I believe amongst the lower classes everywhere, and certainly commendable on the score of simplicity, to silence a woman's objections and aspirations by knocking her down. I have heard it said that this apparently brutal action has anything but the maddening effect tenderly nurtured persons might suppose, and that the patient is soothed and satisfied with a rapidity and completeness unattainable by other and more polite methods. Do you suppose,' he went on, flicking a twig off a tree

107

with his whip as we passed, 'that the intellectual husband, wrestling intellectually with the chaotic yearnings of his intellectual wife, ever achieves the result aimed at? He may and does go on wrestling till he is tired, but never does he in the very least convince her of her folly; while his brother in the ragged coat has got through the whole business in less time than it takes me to speak about it. There is no doubt that these poor women fulfil their vocation far more thoroughly than the women in our class, and, as the truest: happiness consists in finding one's vocation quickly and continuing in it all one's days, I consider they are to be envied rather than not, since they are early taught, by the impossibility of argument with marital muscle, the impotence of female endeavour and the blessings of content.'

'Pray go on,' I said politely.

'These women accept their beatings with a simplicity worthy of all praise, and far from considering themselves insulted, admire the strength and energy of the man who can administer such eloquent rebukes. In Russia, not only may a man beat his wife, but it is laid down in the catechism and taught all boys at the time of confirmation as necessary at least once a week, whether she has done anything or not, for the sake of her general health and happiness.'

I thought I observed a tendency in the Man of Wrath rather to gloat over these castigations.

'Pray, my dear man,' I said, pointing with my whip, 'look at that baby moon so innocently peeping at us over the edge of the mist just behind that silver birch; and don't talk so much about women and things you don't understand. What is the use of your bothering about fists and whips and muscles and all the dreadful things invented for the confusion of obstreperous wives? You know you are a civilised husband, and a civilised husband is a creature who has ceased to be a man.'

'And a civilised wife?' he asked, bringing his horse close up beside me and putting his arm round my waist, 'has she ceased to be a woman?'

'I should think so indeed, — she is a goddess, and can never be worshipped and adored enough.'

'It seems to me,' he said, 'that the conversation is growing personal.'

I started off at a canter across the short, springy turf. The Hirschwald is an enchanted place on such an evening, when the mists lie low on the turf, and overhead the delicate, bare branches of the silver birches stand out clear against the soft sky, while the little moon looks down kindly on the damp November world. Where the trees thicken into a wood, the fragrance of the wet earth and rotting leaves kicked up by the horses' hoofs fills my soul with delight. I particularly love that smell, — it brings before me the entire benevolence of Nature, for ever working death and decay, so piteous in themselves, into the means of fresh life and glory, and sending up sweet odours as she works.

★   ★   ★

December 7th. — I have been to England. I went for at least a month and stayed a week in a fog and was blown home again in a gale. Twice I fled before the fogs into the country to see friends with gardens, but it was raining, and except the beautiful lawns (not to be had in the Fatherland) and the infinite possibilities, there was nothing to interest the intelligent and garden-loving foreigner, for the good reason that you cannot be interested in gardens under an umbrella. So I went back to the fogs, and after groping about for a few days more began to long inordinately for Germany. A terrific gale sprang up after I had started, and the journey both by sea and land was full of horrors, the trains in Germany being heated to such an extent that it is next to impossible to sit still, great gusts of hot air coming up under the cushions, the cushions themselves being very hot, and the wretched traveller still hotter.

But when I reached my home and got out of the train into the purest, brightest snow-atmosphere, the air so still that the whole world seemed to be listening, the sky cloudless, the crisp snow sparkling underfoot and on the trees, and a happy row of three beaming babies awaiting me, I was consoled for all my torments, only remembering them enough to wonder why I had gone away at all.

The babies each had a kitten in one hand and an elegant bouquet of pine needles and grass in the other, and what with the due presentation of the bouquets and the struggles of the kittens, the hugging and kissing was much interfered with. Kittens, bouquets, and babies were all somehow squeezed into the sleigh, and off we went with jingling bells and shrieks of delight. 'Directly you comes home the fun begins,' said the May baby, sitting very close to me. 'How the snow purrs!' cried the April baby, as the horses scrunched it up with their feet. The June baby sat loudly singing 'The King of Love my Shepherd is,' and swinging her kitten round by its tail to emphasise the rhythm.

The house, half-buried in the snow, looked the very abode of peace, and I ran through all the rooms, eager to take possession of them again, and feeling as though I had been away for ever. When I got to the library I came to a standstill, — ah, the dear room, what happy times I have spent in it rummaging amongst the books, making plans for my garden, building castles in the air, writing, dreaming, doing nothing! There was a big peat fire blazing half up the chimney, and the old housekeeper had put pots of flowers about, and on the writing-table was a great bunch of violets scenting the room. 'Oh, how good it is to be home again!' I sighed in my satisfaction. The babies clung about my knees, looking up at me with eyes full of love. Outside the dazzling snow and sunshine, inside the bright room and happy faces — I thought of those yellow fogs and shivered. The library is not used by the Man of Wrath; it is neutral ground where we meet in the evenings for an hour before he disappears into his own rooms — a series of very smoky dens in the southeast corner of the house. It looks, I am afraid, rather too gay for an ideal library; and its colouring, white and yellow, is so cheerful as to be almost frivolous. There are white bookcases all round the walls, and there is a great fireplace, and four windows, facing full south, opening on to my most cherished bit of garden, the bit round the sun-dial; so that with so much colour and such a big fire and such floods of sunshine it has anything but a sober air, in spite of the venerable volumes filling the shelves. Indeed, I should never be surprised if they skipped down from their places, and, picking up their leaves, began to dance.

With this room to live in, I can look forward with perfect equanimity to being snowed up for any time Providence thinks proper; and to go into the garden in its snowed-up state is like going into a bath of purity. The first breath on opening the door is so ineffably pure that it makes me gasp, and I feel a black and sinful object in the midst of all the spotlessness. Yesterday I sat out of doors near the sun-dial the whole afternoon, with the thermometer so many degrees below freezing that it will be weeks finding its way up again; but there was no wind, and beautiful sunshine, and I was well wrapped up in furs. I even had tea brought out there, to the astonishment of the menials, and sat till long after the sun had set, enjoying the frosty air. I had to drink the tea very quickly, for it showed a strong inclination to begin to freeze. After the sun had gone down the rooks came home to their nests in the garden with a great fuss and fluttering, and many hesitations and squabbles before they settled on their respective trees. They flew over my head in hundreds with a mighty swish of wings, and when they had arranged themselves comfortably, an intense hush fell upon the garden, and the house began to look like a Christmas card, with its white roof against the clear, pale green of the western sky, and lamplight shining in the windows.

I had been reading a Life of Luther, lent me by our parson, in the intervals between looking round me and being happy. He came one day with the book and begged me to read it, having discovered that my interest in Luther was not as living as it ought to be; so I took it out with me into the garden, because the dullest book takes on a certain saving grace if read out of doors, just as bread and butter, devoid of charm in the drawing-room, is ambrosia eaten under a tree. I read Luther all the afternoon with pauses for refreshing glances at the garden and the sky, and much thankfulness in my heart. His struggles with devils amazed me; and I wondered whether such a day as that, full of grace and the forgiveness of sins, never struck him as something to make him relent even towards devils. He apparently never allowed himself just to be happy. He was a wonderful man, but I am glad I was not his wife.

Our parson is an interesting person, and untiring in his efforts to improve himself. Both he and his wife study whenever they have a spare moment, and there is a tradition that she stirs her puddings with one hand and holds a Latin grammar in the other, the grammar, of course, getting the greater share of her attention. To most German Hausfraus the dinners and the puddings are of paramount importance, and they pride themselves on keeping those parts of their houses that are seen in a state of perpetual and spotless perfection, and this is exceedingly praiseworthy; but, I would humbly inquire, are there not other things even more important? And is not plain living and high thinking better than the other way about? And all too careful making of dinners and dusting of furniture takes a terrible amount of precious time, and — and with shame I confess that my sympathies are all with the pudding and the grammar. It cannot be right to be the slave of one's household gods, and I protest that if my furniture ever annoyed me by wanting to be dusted when I wanted to be doing something else, and there was no one to do the dusting for me, I would cast it all into the nearest bonfire and sit and warm my toes at the flames with great contentment, triumphantly selling my dusters to the very next pedlar who was weak enough to buy them. Parsons' wives have to do the housework and cooking themselves, and are thus not only cooks and housemaids, but if they have children — and they always do have children — they are head and under nurse as well; and besides these trifling duties have a good deal to do with their fruit and vegetable garden, and everything to do with their poultry. This being so, is it not pathetic to find a young woman bravely struggling to learn languages and keep up with her husband? If I were that husband, those puddings would taste sweetest to me that were served with Latin sauce. They are both severely pious, and are for ever engaged in desperate efforts to practise what they preach; than which, as we all know, nothing is more difficult. He works in his parish with the most noble self-devotion, and never loses courage, although his efforts have been several times rewarded by disgusting libels pasted up on the street-corners, thrown under doors, and even fastened to his own garden wall. The peasant hereabouts is past belief low and animal, and a sensitive, intellectual parson among them is really a pearl before swine.

116

For years he has gone on unflinchingly, filled with the most living faith and hope and charity, and I sometimes wonder whether they are any better now in his parish than they were under his predecessor, a man who smoked and drank beer from Monday morning to Saturday night, never did a stroke of work, and often kept the scanty congregation waiting on Sunday afternoons while he finished his postprandial nap. It is discouraging enough to make most men give in, and leave the parish to get to heaven or not as it pleases; but he never seems discouraged, and goes on sacrificing the best part of his life to these people when all his tastes are literary, and all his inclinations towards the life of the student. His convictions drag him out of his little home at all hours to minister to the sick and exhort the wicked; they give him no rest, and never let him feel he has done enough; and when he comes home weary, after a day's wrestling with his parishioners' souls, he is confronted on his doorstep by filthy abuse pasted up on his own front door. He never speaks of these things, but how shall they be hid? Everybody here knows everything that happens before the day is over, and what we have for dinner is of far greater general interest than the most astounding political earthquake. They have a pretty, roomy cottage, and a good bit of ground adjoining the churchyard. His predecessor used to hang out his washing on the tombstones to dry, but then he was a person entirely lost to all sense of decency, and had finally to be removed, preaching a farewell sermon of a most vituperative description, and hurling invective at the Man of Wrath, who sat up in his box drinking in every word and enjoying himself thoroughly. The Man of Wrath likes novelty, and such a sermon had never been heard before. It is spoken of in the village to this day with bated breath and awful joy.

* * *

December 22nd. — Up to now we have had a beautiful winter. Clear skies, frost, little wind, and, except for a sharp touch now and then, very few really cold days. My windows are gay with hyacinths and lilies of the valley; and though, as I have said, I don't admire the smell of hyacinths in the spring when it seems wanting in youth and chastity next to that of other flowers, I am glad enough now to bury my nose in their heavy sweetness. In December one cannot afford to be fastidious; besides, one is actually less fastidious about everything in the winter. The keen air braces soul as well as body into robustness, and the food and the perfume disliked in the summer are perfectly welcome then.

I am very busy preparing for Christmas, but have often locked myself up in a room alone, shutting out my unfinished duties, to study the flower catalogues and make my lists of seeds and shrubs and trees for the spring. It is a fascinating occupation, and acquires an additional charm when you know you ought to be doing something else, that Christmas is at the door, that children and servants and farm hands depend on you for their pleasure, and that, if you don't see to the decoration of the trees and house, and the buying of the presents, nobody else will. The hours fly by shut up with those catalogues and with Duty snarling on the other side of the door. I don't like Duty — everything in the least disagreeable is always sure to be one's duty. Why cannot it be my duty to make lists and plans for the dear garden? 'And so it is,' I insisted to the Man of Wrath, when he protested against what he called wasting my time upstairs. 'No,' he replied sagely; 'your garden is not your duty, because it is your Pleasure.'

What a comfort it is to have such wells of wisdom constantly at my disposal! Anybody can have a husband, but to few is it given to have a sage, and the combination of both is as rare as it is useful. Indeed, in its practical utility the only thing I ever saw to equal it is a sofa my neighbour has bought as a Christmas surprise for her husband, and which she showed me the last time I called there — a beautiful invention, as she explained, combining a bedstead, a sofa, and a chest of drawers, and into which you put your clothes, and on top of which you put yourself, and if anybody calls in the middle of the night and you happen to be using the drawing-room as a bedroom, you just pop the bedclothes inside, and there you are discovered sitting on your sofa and looking for all the world as though you had been expecting visitors for hours.

'Pray, does he wear pyjamas?' I inquired.

But she had never heard of pyjamas.

It takes a long time to make my spring lists. I want to have a border all yellow, every shade of yellow from fieriest orange to nearly white, and the amount of work and studying of gardening books it costs me will only be appreciated by beginners like myself. I have been weeks planning it, and it is not nearly finished. I want it to be a succession of glories from May till the frosts, and the chief feature is to be the number of 'ardent marigolds' — flowers that I very tenderly love — and nasturtiums. The nasturtiums are to be of every sort and shade, and are to climb and creep and grow in bushes, and show their lovely flowers and leaves to the best advantage. Then there are to be eschscholtzias, dahlias, sunflowers, zinnias, scabiosa, portulaca, yellow violas, yellow stocks, yellow sweet-peas, yellow lupins — everything that is yellow or that has a yellow variety. The place I have chosen for it is a long, wide border in the sun, at the foot of a grassy slope crowned with lilacs and pines, and facing southeast. You go through a little pine wood, and, turning a corner, are to come suddenly upon this bit of captured morning glory. I want it to be blinding in its brightness after the dark, cool path through the wood.

That is the idea. Depression seizes me when I reflect upon the probable difference between the idea and its realisation. I am ignorant, and the gardener is, I do believe, still more so; for he was forcing some tulips, and they have all shrivelled up and died, and he says he cannot imagine why. Besides, he is in love with the cook, and is going to marry her after Christmas, and refuses to enter into any of my plans with the enthusiasm they deserve, but sits with vacant eye dreamily chopping wood from morning till night to keep the beloved one's kitchen fire well supplied. I cannot understand anyone preferring cooks to marigolds; those future marigolds, shadowy as they are, and whose seeds are still sleeping at the seedsman's, have shone through my winter days like golden lamps.

I wish with all my heart I were a man, for of course the first thing I should do would be to buy a spade and go and garden, and then I should have the delight of doing everything for my flowers with my own hands and need not waste time explaining what I want done to somebody else. It is dull work giving orders and trying to describe the bright visions of one's brain to a person who has no visions and no brain, and who thinks a yellow bed should be calceolarias edged with blue.

I have taken care in choosing my yellow plants to put down only those humble ones that are easily pleased and grateful for little, for my soil is by no means all that it might be, and to most plants the climate is rather trying. I feel really grateful to any flower that is sturdy and willing enough to flourish here. Pansies seem to like the place and so do sweet-peas; pinks don't, and after much coaxing gave hardly any flowers last summer. Nearly all the roses were a success, in spite of the sandy soil, except the tea-rose Adam, which was covered with buds ready to open, when they suddenly turned brown and died, and three standard Dr. Grills which stood in a row and simply sulked. I had been very excited about Dr. Grill, his description in the catalogues being specially fascinating, and no doubt I deserved the snubbing I got. 'Never be excited, my dears, about anything,' shall be the advice I will give the three babies when the time comes to take them out to parties, 'or, if you are, don't show it. If by nature you are volcanoes, at least be only smouldering ones. Don't look pleased, don't look interested, don't, above all things, look eager. Calm indifference should be written on every feature of your faces. Never show that you like any one person, or any one thing. Be cool, languid, and reserved. If you don't do as your mother tells you and are just gushing, frisky, young idiots, snubs will be your portion. If you do as she tells you, you'll marry princes and live happily ever after.'

Dr. Grill must be a German rose. In this part of the world the more you are pleased to see a person the less is he pleased to see you; whereas, if you are disagreeable, he will grow pleasant visibly, his countenance expanding into wider amiability the more your own is stiff and sour. But I was not prepared for that sort of thing in a rose, and was disgusted with Dr. Grill. He had the best place in the garden — warm, sunny, and sheltered; his holes were prepared with the tenderest care; he was given the most dainty mixture of compost, clay, and manure; he was watered assiduously all through the drought when more willing flowers got nothing; and he refused to do anything but look black and shrivel. He did not die, but neither did he live — he just existed; and at the end of the summer not one of him had a scrap more shoot or leaf than when he was first put in in April. It would have been better if he had died straight away, for then I should have known what to do; as it is, there he is still occupying the best place, wrapped up carefully for the winter, excluding kinder roses, and probably intending to repeat the same conduct next year. Well, trials are the portion of mankind, and gardeners have their share, and in any case it is better to be tried by plants than persons, seeing that with plants you know that it is you who are in the wrong, and with persons it is always the other way about — and who is there among us who has not felt the pangs of injured innocence, and known them to be grievous?

I have two visitors staying with me, though I have done nothing to provoke such an infliction, and had been looking forward to a happy little Christmas alone with the Man of Wrath and the babies. Fate decreed otherwise. Quite regularly, if I look forward to anything, Fate steps in and decrees otherwise;

I don't know why it should, but it does. I had not even invited these good ladies — like greatness on the modest, they were thrust upon me. One is Irais, the sweet singer of the summer, whom I love as she deserves, but of whom I certainly thought I had seen the last for at least a year, when she wrote and asked if I would have her over Christmas, as her husband was out of sorts, and she didn't like him in that state. Neither do I like sick husbands, so, full of sympathy, I begged her to come, and here she is. And the other is Minora.

Why I have to have Minora I don't know, for I was not even aware of her existence a fortnight ago. Then coming down cheerfully one morning to breakfast — it was the very day after my return from England — I found a letter from an English friend, who up till then had been perfectly innocuous, asking me to befriend Minora. I read the letter aloud for the benefit of the Man of Wrath, who was eating Spickgans, a delicacy much sought after in these parts. 'Do, my dear Elizabeth,' wrote my friend, 'take some notice of the poor thing. She is studying art in Dresden, and has nowhere literally to go for Christmas. She is very ambitious and hardworking — '

'Then,' interrupted the Man of Wrath, 'she is not pretty. Only ugly girls work hard.'

' — and she is really very clever — '

'I do not like clever girls, they are so stupid,' again interrupted the Man of Wrath.

' — and unless some kind creature like yourself takes pity on her she will be very lonely.'

'Then let her be lonely.'

'Her mother is my oldest friend, and would be greatly distressed to think that her daughter should be alone in a foreign town at such a season.'

'I do not mind the distress of the mother.'

'Oh, dear me,' I exclaimed impatiently, 'I shall have to ask her to come!'

'If you should be inclined,' the letter went on, 'to play the good Samaritan, dear Elizabeth, I am positive you would find Minora a bright, intelligent companion — '

'Minora?' questioned the Man of Wrath.

The April baby, who has had a nursery governess of an altogether alarmingly zealous type attached to her person for the last six weeks, looked up from her bread and milk.

'It sounds like islands,' she remarked pensively.

The governess coughed.

'Majora, Minora, Alderney, and Sark,' explained her pupil.

I looked at her severely.

'If you are not careful, April,' I said, 'you'll

126

be a genius when you grow up and disgrace your parents.'

Miss Jones looked as though she did not like Germans. I am afraid she despises us because she thinks we are foreigners — an attitude of mind quite British and wholly to her credit; but we, on the other hand, regard her as a foreigner, which, of course, makes things complicated.

'Shall I really have to have this strange girl?' I asked, addressing nobody in particular and not expecting a reply.

'You need not have her,' said the Man of Wrath composedly, 'but you will. You will write to-day and cordially invite her, and when she has been here twenty-four hours you will quarrel with her. I know you, my dear.'

'Quarrel! I? With a little art-student?' Miss Jones cast down her eyes. She is perpetually scenting a scene, and is always ready to bring whole batteries of discretion and tact and good taste to bear on us, and seems to know we are disputing in an unseemly manner when we would never dream it ourselves but for the warning of her downcast eyes. I would take my courage in both hands and ask her to go, for besides this superfluity of discreet behaviour she is, although only nursery, much too zealous, and inclined to be always teaching and never playing; but, unfortunately, the April baby adores her and is sure there never was any one so beautiful before. She comes every day with fresh accounts of the splendours of her wardrobe, and feeling descriptions of her umbrellas and hats; and Miss Jones looks offended and purses up her lips. In common with most governesses, she has a little dark down on her upper lip, and the April baby appeared one day at dinner with her own decorated in faithful imitation, having achieved it after much struggling, with the aid of a lead pencil and unbounded love. Miss Jones put her in the corner for impertinence. I wonder why governesses are so unpleasant. The Man of Wrath says it is because they are not married. Without venturing to differ entirely from the opinion of experience, I would add that the strain of continually having to set an example must surely be very great. It is much easier, and often more pleasant, to be a warning than an example, and governesses are but women, and women are sometimes foolish, and when you want to be foolish it must be annoying to have to be wise.

Minora and Irais arrived yesterday together; or rather, when the carriage drove up, Irais got out of it alone, and informed me that there was a strange girl on a bicycle a little way behind.

I sent back the carriage to pick her up, for it was dusk and the roads are terrible.

'But why do you have strange girls here at all?' asked Irais rather peevishly, taking off her hat in the library before the fire, and otherwise making herself very much at home; 'I don't like them. I'm not sure that they're not worse than husbands who are out of order. Who is she? She would bicycle from the station, and is, I am sure, the first woman who has done it. The little boys threw stones at her.'

'Oh, my dear, that only shows the ignorance of the little boys. Never mind her. Let us have tea in peace before she comes.' 'But we should be much happier without her,' she grumbled. 'Weren't we happy enough in the summer, Elizabeth — just you and I?'

'Yes, indeed we were,' I answered heartily, putting my arms round her. The flame of my affection for Irais burns very brightly on the day of her arrival; besides, this time I have prudently provided against her sinning with the salt-cellars by ordering them to be handed round like vegetable dishes. We had finished tea and she had gone up to her room to dress before Minora and her bicycle were got here. I hurried out to meet her, feeling sorry for her, plunged into a circle of strangers at such a very personal season as Christmas. But she was not very shy; indeed, she was less shy than I was, and lingered in the hall, giving the servants directions to wipe the snow off the tyres of her machine before she lent an attentive ear to my welcoming remarks.

'I couldn't make your man understand me at the station,' she said at last, when her mind was at rest about her bicycle; 'I asked him how far it was, and what the roads were like, and he only smiled. Is he German? But of course he is — how odd that he didn't understand. You speak English very well, — very well indeed, do you know.' By this time we were in the library, and she stood on the hearth-rug warming her back while I poured her out some tea.

'What a quaint room,' she remarked, looking round, 'and the hall is so curious too. Very old, isn't it? There's a lot of copy here.'

The Man of Wrath, who had been in the hall on her arrival and had come in with us, began to look about on the carpet. 'Copy' he inquired, 'Where's copy?'

'Oh — material, you know, for a book. I'm just jotting down what strikes me in your country, and when I have time shall throw it into book form.' She spoke very loud, as English people always do to foreigners.

'My dear,' I said breathlessly to Irais, when

I had got into her room and shut the door and Minora was safely in hers, 'what do you think — she writes books!'

'What — the bicycling girl?'

'Yes — Minora — imagine it!'

We stood and looked at each other with awestruck faces.

'How dreadful!' murmured Irais. 'I never met a young girl who did that before.'

'She says this place is full of copy.'

'Full of what?'

'That's what you make books with.'

'Oh, my dear, this is worse than I expected! A strange girl is always a bore among good friends, but one can generally manage her. But a girl who writes books — why, it isn't respectable! And you can't snub that sort of people; they're unsnubbable.'

'Oh, but we'll try!' I cried, with such heartiness that we both laughed.

The hall and the library struck Minora most; indeed, she lingered so long after dinner in the hall, which is cold, that the Man of Wrath put on his fur coat by way of a gentle hint. His hints are always gentle.

She wanted to hear the whole story about the chapel and the nuns and Gustavus Adolphus, and pulling out a fat note-book began to take down what I said. I at once relapsed into silence.

'Well?' she said.

'That's all.'

'Oh, but you've only just begun.'

'It doesn't go any further. Won't you come into the library?'

In the library she again took up her stand before the fire and warmed herself, and we sat in a row and were cold. She has a wonderfully good profile, which is irritating. The wind, however, is tempered to the shorn lamb by her eyes being set too closely together.

Irais lit a cigarette, and leaning back in her chair, contemplated her critically beneath her long eyelashes. 'You are writing a book?' she asked presently.

'Well — yes, I suppose I may say that I am. Just my impressions, you know, of your country. Anything that strikes me as curious or amusing — I jot it down, and when I have time shall work it up into something, I daresay.'

'Are you not studying painting?'

'Yes, but I can't study that for ever. We have an English proverb: 'Life is short and Art is long' — too long, I sometimes think — and writing is a great relaxation when I am tired.'

'What shall you call it?'

'Oh, I thought of calling it Journeyings in Germany. It sounds well, and would be correct. Or Jottings from German Journey-ings, — I haven't quite decided yet which.'

'By the author of Prowls in Pomerania, you might add,' suggested Irais.

'And Drivel from Dresden,' said I.

'And Bosh from Berlin,' added Irais.

Minora stared. 'I don't think those two last ones would do,' she said, 'because it is not to be a facetious book. But your first one is rather a good title,' she added, looking at Irais and drawing out her note-book. 'I think I'll just jot that down.'

'If you jot down all we say and then publish it, will it still be your book?' asked Irais.

But Minora was so busy scribbling that she did not hear.

'And have you no suggestions to make, Sage?' asked Irais, turning to the Man of Wrath, who was blowing out clouds of smoke in silence.

'Oh, do you call him Sage?' cried Minora; 'and always in English?'

Irais and I looked at each other. We knew what we did call him, and were afraid Minora would in time ferret it out and enter it in her note-book. The Man of Wrath looked none too well pleased to be alluded to under his very nose by our new guest as 'him.'

'Husbands are always sages,' said I gravely.

'Though sages are not always husbands,'

said Irais with equal gravity. 'Sages and husbands — sage and husbands — ' she went on musingly, 'what does that remind you of, Miss Minora?'

'Oh, I know, — how stupid of me!' cried Minora eagerly, her pencil in mid-air and her brain clutching at the elusive recollection, 'sage and, — why, — yes, — no, — yes, of course — oh,' disappointedly, 'but that's vulgar — I can't put it in.'

'What is vulgar?' I asked.

'She thinks sage and onions is vulgar,' said Irais languidly; 'but it isn't, it is very good.' She got up and walked to the piano, and, sitting down, began, after a little wandering over the keys, to sing.

'Do you play?' I asked Minora.

'Yes, but I am afraid I am rather out of practice.'

I said no more. I know what that sort of playing is.

When we were lighting our bedroom candles Minora began suddenly to speak in an unknown tongue. We stared. 'What is the matter with her?' murmured Irais.

'I thought, perhaps,' said Minora in English, 'you might prefer to talk German, and as it is all the same to me what I talk — '

'Oh, pray don't trouble,' said Irais. 'We like airing our English — don't we, Elizabeth?'

'I don't want my German to get rusty though,' said Minora; 'I shouldn't like to forget it.'

'Oh, but isn't there an English song,' said Irais, twisting round her neck as she preceded us upstairs, ' "'Tis folly to remember, 'tis wisdom to forget"?'

'You are not nervous sleeping alone, I hope,' I said hastily.

'What room is she in?' asked Irais.

'No. 12.'

'Oh! — do you believe in ghosts?'

Minora turned pale.

'What nonsense,' said I; 'we have no ghosts here. Good-night. If you want anything, mind you ring.'

'And if you see anything curious in that room,' called Irais from her bedroom door, 'mind you jot it down.'

★ ★ ★

December 27th — It is the fashion, I believe, to regard Christmas as a bore of rather a gross description, and as a time when you are invited to over-eat yourself, and pretend to be merry without just cause. As a matter of fact, it is one of the prettiest and most poetic institutions possible, if observed in the proper manner, and after having been more or less unpleasant to everybody for a whole year, it is a blessing to be forced on that one day to be amiable, and it is certainly delightful to be able to give presents without being haunted by the conviction that you are spoiling the recipient, and will suffer for it afterward. Servants are only big children, and are made just as happy as children by little presents and nice things to eat, and, for days beforehand, every time the three babies go into the garden they expect to meet the Christ Child with His arms full of gifts. They firmly believe that it is thus their presents are brought, and it is such a charming idea that Christmas would be worth celebrating for its sake alone.

As great secrecy is observed, the preparations devolve entirely on me, and it is not very easy work, with so many people in our own house and on each of the farms, and all the children, big and little, expecting their share of happiness. The library is uninhabitable for several days before and after, as it is there that we have the trees and presents. All down one side are the trees, and the other three sides are lined with tables, a separate one for each person in the house. When the trees are lighted, and stand in their radiance shining down on the happy faces, I forget all the trouble it has been, and the number of times I have had to run up and down stairs, and the various aches in head and feet, and enjoy myself as much as anybody. First the June baby is ushered in, then the others and ourselves according to age, then the servants, then come the head inspector and his family, the other inspectors from the different farms, the mamsells, the bookkeepers and secretaries, and then all the children, troops and troops of them — the big ones leading the little ones by the hand and carrying the babies in their arms, and the mothers peeping round the door. As many as can get in stand in front of the trees, and sing two or three carols; then they are given their presents, and go off triumphantly, making room for the next batch. My three babies sang lustily too, whether they happened to know what was being sung or not. They had on white dresses in honour of the occasion, and the June baby was even arrayed in a low-necked and short-sleeved garment, after the manner of Teutonic infants, whatever the state of the thermometer. Her arms are like miniature prize-fighter's arms — I never saw such things; they are the pride and joy of her little nurse, who had tied them up with blue ribbons, and kept on kissing them. I shall certainly not be able to take her to balls when she grows up, if she goes on having arms like that.

When they came to say good-night, they were all very pale and subdued. The April baby had an exhausted-looking Japanese doll with her, which she said she was taking to bed, not because she liked him, but because she was so sorry for him, he seemed so very tired. They kissed me absently, and went away, only the April baby glancing at the trees as she passed and making them a curtesy.

'Good-bye, trees,' I heard her say; and then she made the Japanese doll bow to them, which he did, in a very languid and blasé fashion. 'You'll never see such trees again,' she told him, giving him a vindictive shake, 'for you'll be brokened long before next time.'

She went out, but came back as though she had forgotten something.

'Thank the Christkind so much, Mummy, won't you, for all the lovely things He brought us. I suppose you're writing to Him now, isn't you?'

I cannot see that there was anything gross about our Christmas, and we were perfectly merry without any need to pretend, and for at least two days it brought us a little nearer together, and made us kind. Happiness is so wholesome; it invigorates and warms me into piety far more effectually than any amount of trials and griefs, and an unexpected pleasure is the surest means of bringing me to my knees. In spite of the protestations of some peculiarly constructed persons that they are the better for trials, I don't believe it. Such things must sour us, just as happiness must sweeten us, and make us kinder, and more gentle. And will anybody affirm that it behoves us to be more thankful for trials than for blessings? We were meant to be happy, and to accept all the happiness offered with thankfulness — indeed, we are none of us ever thankful enough, and yet we each get so much, so very much, more than we deserve. I know a woman — she stayed with me last summer — who rejoices grimly when those she loves suffer. She believes that it is our lot, and that it braces us and does us good, and she would shield no one from even unnecessary pain; she weeps with the sufferer, but is convinced it is all for the best. Well, let her continue in her dreary beliefs; she has no garden to teach her the beauty and the happiness of holiness, nor does she in the least desire to possess one; her convictions have the sad gray colouring of the dingy streets and houses she lives amongst — the sad colour of humanity in masses. Submission to what people call their 'lot' is simply ignoble. If your lot makes you cry and be wretched, get rid of it and take another; strike out for yourself; don't listen to the shrieks of your relations, to their gibes or their entreaties; don't let your own microscopic set prescribe your goings-out and comings-in; don't be afraid of public opinion in the shape of the neighbour in the next house, when all the world is before you new and shining, and everything is possible, if you will only be energetic and independent and seize opportunity by the scruff of the neck.

'To hear you talk,' said Irais, 'no one would ever imagine that you dream away your days in a garden with a book, and that you never in your life seized anything by the scruff of its neck. And what is scruff? I hope I have not got any on me.' And she craned her neck before the glass.

She and Minora were going to help me decorate the trees, but very soon Irais wandered off to the piano, and Minora was tired and took up a book; so I called in Miss Jones and the babies — it was Miss Jones's last public appearance, as I shall relate — and after working for the best part of two days they were finished, and looked like lovely ladies in widespreading, sparkling petticoats, holding up their skirts with glittering fingers. Minora wrote a long description of them for a chapter of her book which is headed Noel, — I saw that much, because she left it open on the table while she went to talk to Miss Jones. They were fast friends from the very first, and though it is said to be natural to take to one's own countrymen, I am unable altogether to sympathise with such a reason for sudden affection.

'I wonder what they talk about?' I said to Irais yesterday, when there was no getting Minora to come to tea, so deeply was she engaged in conversation with Miss Jones.

'Oh, my dear, how can I tell? Lovers, I suppose, or else they think they are clever, and then they talk rubbish.'

'Well, of course, Minora thinks she is clever.'

'I suppose she does. What does it matter what she thinks? Why does your governess look so gloomy? When I see her at luncheon I always imagine she must have just heard that somebody is dead. But she can't hear that every day. What is the matter with her?'

'I don't think she feels quite as proper as she looks,' I said doubtfully; I was for ever trying to account for Miss Jones's expression.

'But that must be rather nice,' said Irais. 'It would be awful for her if she felt exactly the same as she looks.'

At that moment the door leading into the schoolroom opened softly, and the April baby, tired of playing, came in and sat down at my feet, leaving the door open; and this is what we heard Miss Jones saying —

'Parents are seldom wise, and the strain the conscientious place upon themselves to appear so before their children and governess must be terrible. Nor are clergymen more pious than other men, yet they have continually to pose before their flock as such. As for governesses, Miss Minora, I know what I am saying when I affirm that there is nothing more intolerable than to have to be polite, and even humble, to persons whose weaknesses and follies are glaringly apparent in every word they utter, and to be forced by the presence of children and employers to a dignity of manner in no way corresponding to one's feelings. The grave father of a family, who was probably one of the least respectable of bachelors, is an interesting study at his own table, where he is constrained to assume airs of infallibility merely because his children are looking at him. The fact of his being a parent does not endow him with any supreme and sudden virtue; and I can assure you that among the eyes fixed upon him, not the least critical and amused are those of the humble person who fills the post of governess.'

'Oh, Miss Jones, how lovely!' we heard Minora say in accents of rapture, while we sat transfixed with horror at these sentiments. 'Do you mind if I put that down in my book? You say it all so beautifully.'

'Without a few hours of relaxation,' continued Miss Jones, 'of private indemnification for the toilsome virtues displayed in public, who could wade through days of correct behaviour? There would be no reaction, no room for better impulses, no place for repentance. Parents, priests, and governesses would be in the situation of a stout lady who never has a quiet moment in which she can take off her corsets.'

'My dear, what a firebrand!' whispered Irais. I got up and went in. They were sitting on the sofa, Minora with clasped hands, gazing admiringly into Miss Jones's face, which wore a very different expression from the one of sour and unwilling propriety I have been used to seeing.

'May I ask you to come to tea?' I said to Minora. 'And I should like to have the children a little while.'

She got up very reluctantly, but I waited with the door open until she had gone in and the two babies had followed. They had been playing at stuffing each other's ears with pieces of newspaper while Miss Jones provided Minora with noble thoughts for her work, and had to be tortured afterward with tweezers. I said nothing to Minora, but kept her with us till dinner-time, and this morning we went for a long sleigh-drive. When we came in to lunch there was no Miss Jones.

'Is Miss Jones ill?' asked Minora.

'She is gone,' I said.

'Gone?'

'Did you never hear of such things as sick mothers?' asked Irais blandly; and we talked resolutely of something else.

All the afternoon Minora has moped. She had found a kindred spirit, and it has been ruthlessly torn from her arms as kindred spirits so often are. It is enough to make her mope, and it is not her fault, poor thing, that she should have preferred the society of a Miss Jones to that of Irais and myself.

At dinner Irais surveyed her with her head on one side. 'You look so pale,' she said; 'are you not well?'

Minora raised her eyes heavily, with the patient air of one who likes to be thought a sufferer. 'I have a slight headache,' she replied gently.

'I hope you are not going to be ill,' said Irais with great concern, 'because there is only a cow-doctor to be had here, and though he means well, I believe he is rather rough.' Minora was plainly startled. 'But what do you do if you are ill?' she asked.

'Oh, we are never ill,' said I; 'the very knowledge that there would be no one to cure us seems to keep us healthy.'

'And if any one takes to her bed,' said Irais, 'Elizabeth always calls in the cow-doctor.'

Minora was silent. She feels, I am sure, that

she has got into a part of the world peopled solely by barbarians, and that the only civilised creature besides herself has departed and left her at our mercy. Whatever her reflections may be her symptoms are visibly abating.

★　★　★

January 1st. — The service on New Year's Eve is the only one in the whole year that in the least impresses me in our little church, and then the very bareness and ugliness of the place and the ceremonial produce an effect that a snug service in a well-lit church never would. Last night we took Irais and Minora, and drove the three lonely miles in a sleigh. It was pitch-dark, and blowing great guns. We sat wrapped up to our eyes in furs, and as mute as a funeral procession.

'We are going to the burial of our last year's sins,' said Irais, as we started; and there certainly was a funereal sort of feeling in the air. Up in our gallery pew we tried to decipher our chorales by the light of the spluttering tallow candles stuck in holes in the woodwork, the flames wildly blown about by the draughts. The wind banged against the windows in great gusts, screaming louder than the organ, and threatening to blow out the agitated lights together. The parson in his gloomy pulpit, surrounded by a framework of dusty carved angels, took on an awful appearance of menacing Authority as he raised his voice to make himself heard above the clatter. Sitting there in the dark, I felt very small, and solitary, and defenceless, alone in a great, big, black world. The church was as cold as a tomb; some of the candles guttered and went out; the parson in his black robe spoke of death and judgment; I thought I heard a child's voice screaming, and could hardly believe it was only the wind, and felt uneasy and full of forebodings; all my faith and philosophy deserted me, and I had a horrid feeling that I should probably be well punished, though for what I had no precise idea. If it had not been so dark, and if the wind had not howled so despairingly, I should have paid little attention to the threats issuing from the pulpit; but, as it was, I fell to making good resolutions. This is always a bad sign, — only those who break them make them; and if you simply do as a matter of course that which is right as it comes, any preparatory resolving to do so becomes completely superfluous. I have for some years past left off making them on New Year's Eve, and only the gale happening as it did reduced me to doing so last night; for I have long since discovered that, though the year and the resolutions may be new, I myself am not, and it is worse than useless putting new wine into old bottles.

'But I am not an old bottle,' said Irais indignantly, when I held forth to her to the above effect a few hours later in the library, restored to all my philosophy by the warmth and light, 'and I find my resolutions carry me very nicely into the spring. I revise them at the end of each month, and strike out the unnecessary ones. By the end of April they have been so severely revised that there are none left.'

'There, you see I am right; if you were not an old bottle your new contents would gradually arrange themselves amiably as a part of you, and the practice of your resolutions would lose its bitterness by becoming a habit.'

She shook her head. 'Such things never lose their bitterness,' she said, 'and that is why I don't let them cling to me right into the summer. When May comes, I give myself up to jollity with all the rest of the world, and am too busy being happy to bother about anything I may have resolved when the days were cold and dark.'

'And that is just why I love you,' I thought. She often says what I feel.

'I wonder,' she went on after a pause, 'whether men ever make resolutions?'

'I don't think they do. Only women indulge in such luxuries. It is a nice sort of feeling, when you have nothing else to do, giving way to endless grief and penitence, and steeping yourself to the eyes in contrition; but it is silly. Why cry over things that are done? Why do naughty things at all, if you are going to repent afterward? Nobody is naughty unless they like being naughty; and nobody ever really repents unless they are afraid they are going to be found out.'

'By 'nobody' of course you mean women,' said Irais.

'Naturally; the terms are synonymous. Besides, men generally have the courage of their opinions.'

'I hope you are listening, Miss Minora,' said Irais in the amiably polite tone she assumes whenever she speaks to that young person.

It was getting on towards midnight, and we were sitting round the fire, waiting for the New Year, and sipping Glühwein, prepared at a small table by the Man of Wrath. It was hot, and sweet, and rather nasty, but it is proper to drink it on this one night, so of course we did.

Minora does not like either Irais or myself. We very soon discovered that, and laugh about it when we are alone together. I can understand her disliking Irais, but she must be a perverse creature not to like me. Irais has poked fun at her, and I have been, I hope, very kind; yet we are bracketed together in her black books. It is also apparent that she looks upon the Man of Wrath as an interesting example of an ill-used and misunderstood husband, and she is disposed to take him under her wing, and defend him on all occasions against us. He never speaks to her; he is at all times a man of few words, but, as far as Minora is concerned, he might have no tongue at all, and sits sphinx-like and impenetrable while she takes us to task about some remark of a profane nature that we may have addressed to him. One night, some days after her arrival, she developed a skittishness of manner which has since disappeared, and tried to be playful with him; but you might as well try to be playful with a graven image. The wife of one of the servants had just produced a boy, the first after a series of five daughters, and at dinner we drank the health of all parties concerned, the Man of Wrath making the happy father drink a glass off at one gulp, his heels well together in military fashion. Minora thought the incident typical of German manners, and not only made notes about it, but joined heartily in the health-drinking, and afterward grew skittish.

She proposed, first of all, to teach us a dance called, I think, the Washington Post, and which was, she said, much danced in England; and, to induce us to learn, she played the tune to us on the piano. We remained untouched by its beauties, each buried in an easy-chair toasting our toes at the fire. Amongst those toes were those of the Man of Wrath, who sat peaceably reading a book and smoking. Minora volunteered to show us the steps, and as we still did not move, danced solitary behind our chairs. Irais did not even turn her head to look, and I was the only one amiable or polite enough to do so. Do I deserve to be placed in Minora's list of disagreeable people side by side with Irais? Certainly not. Yet I most surely am.

'It wants the music, of course,' observed Minora breathlessly, darting in and out between the chairs, apparently addressing me, but glancing at the Man of Wrath.

No answer from anybody.

'It is such a pretty dance,' she panted again, after a few more gyrations.

No answer.

'And is all the rage at home.'

No answer.

'Do let me teach you. Won't you try, Herr Sage?'

She went up to him and dropped him a little curtsey. It is thus she always addresses him, entirely oblivious to the fact, so patent to every one else, that he resents it.

'Oh come, put away that tiresome old book,' she went on gaily, as he did not move; 'I am certain it is only some dry agricultural work that you just nod over. Dancing is much better for you.' Irais and I looked at one another quite frightened. I am sure we both turned pale when the unhappy girl actually laid hold forcibly of his book, and, with a playful little shriek, ran away with it into the next room, hugging it to her bosom and looking back roguishly over her shoulder at him as she ran. There was an awful pause. We hardly dared raise our eyes. Then the Man of Wrath got up slowly, knocked the ashes off the end of his cigar, looked at his watch, and went out at the opposite door into his own rooms, where he stayed for the rest of the evening. She has never, I must say, been skittish since.

'I hope you are listening, Miss Minora,' said Irais, 'because this sort of conversation is likely to do you good.'

'I always listen when people talk sensibly,' replied Minora, stirring her grog.

Irais glanced at her with slightly doubtful eyebrows. 'Do you agree with our hostess's

151

description of women?' she asked after a pause.

'As nobodies? No, of course I do not.'

'Yet she is right. In the eye of the law we are literally nobodies in our country. Did you know that women are forbidden to go to political meetings here?'

'Really?' Out came the note-book.

'The law expressly forbids the attendance at such meetings of women, children, and idiots.'

'Children and idiots — I understand that,' said Minora; 'but women — and classed with children and idiots?'

'Classed with children and idiots,' repeated Irais, gravely nodding her head. 'Did you know that the law forbids females of any age to ride on the top of omnibuses or tramcars?'

'Not really?'

'Do you know why?'

'I can't imagine.'

'Because in going up and down the stairs those inside might perhaps catch a glimpse of the stocking covering their ankles.'

'But what — '

'Did you know that the morals of the German public are in such a shaky condition that a glimpse of that sort would be fatal to them?'

'But I don't see how a stocking — '

'With stripes round it,' said Irais.

'And darns in it,' I added, ' — could possibly be pernicious?'

' "The Pernicious Stocking; or, Thoughts on the Ethics of Petticoats," ' said Irais. 'Put that down as the name of your next book on Germany.'

'I never know,' complained Minora, letting her note-book fall, 'whether you are in earnest or not.'

'Don't you?' said Irais sweetly.

'Is it true,' appealed Minora to the Man of Wrath, busy with his lemons in the background, 'that your law classes women with children and idiots?'

'Certainly,' he answered promptly, 'and a very proper classification, too.'

We all looked blank. 'That's rude,' said I at last.

'Truth is always rude, my dear,' he replied complacently. Then he added, 'If I were commissioned to draw up a new legal code, and had previously enjoyed the privilege, as I have been doing lately, of listening to the conversation of you three young ladies, I should make precisely the same classification.'

Even Minora was incensed at this.

'You are telling us in the most unvarnished manner that we are idiots,' said Irais.

'Idiots? No, no, by no means. But children,

— nice little agreeable children. I very much like to hear you talk together. It is all so young and fresh what you think and what you believe, and not of the least consequence to any one.

'Not of the least consequence?' cried Minora. 'What we believe is of very great consequence indeed to us.'

'Are you jeering at our beliefs?' inquired Irais sternly.

'Not for worlds. I would not on any account disturb or change your pretty little beliefs. It is your chief charm that you always believe every-thing. How desperate would our case be if young ladies only believed facts, and never accepted another person's assurance, but preferred the evidence of their own eyes! They would have no illusions, and a woman without illusions is the dreariest and most difficult thing to manage possible.'

'Thing?' protested Irais.

The Man of Wrath, usually so silent, makes up for it from time to time by holding forth at unnecessary length. He took up his stand now with his back to the fire, and a glass of Glühwein in his hand. Minora had hardly heard his voice before, so quiet had he been since she came, and sat with her pencil raised, ready to fix for ever the wisdom that should flow from his lips.

154

'What would become of poetry if women became so sensible that they turned a deaf ear to the poetic platitudes of love? That love does indulge in platitudes I suppose you will admit.' He looked at Irais.

'Yes, they all say exactly the same thing,' she acknowledged.

'Who could murmur pretty speeches on the beauty of a common sacrifice, if the listener's want of imagination was such as to enable her only to distinguish one victim in the picture, and that one herself?'

Minora took that down word for word, — much good may it do her.

'Who would be brave enough to affirm that if refused he will die, if his assurances merely elicit a recommendation to diet himself, and take plenty of outdoor exercise? Women are responsible for such lies, because they believe them. Their amazing vanity makes them swallow flattery so gross that it is an insult, and men will always be ready to tell the precise number of lies that a woman is ready to listen to. Who indulges more recklessly in glowing exaggerations than the lover who hopes, and has not yet obtained? He will, like the nightingale, sing with unceasing modulations, display all his talent, untiringly repeat his sweetest notes, until he has what he wants, when his song, like the nightingale's,

155

immediately ceases, never again to be heard.'

'Take that down,' murmured Irais aside to Minora — unnecessary advice, for her pencil was scribbling as fast as it could.

'A woman's vanity is so immeasurable that, after having had ninety-nine object-lessons in the difference between promise and performance and the emptiness of pretty speeches, the beginning of the hundredth will find her lending the same willing and enchanted ear to the eloquence of flattery as she did on the occasion of the first. What can the exhortations of the strong-minded sister, who has never had these experiences, do for such a woman? It is useless to tell her she is man's victim, that she is his plaything, that she is cheated, down-trodden, kept under, laughed at, shabbily treated in every way — that is not a true statement of the case. She is simply the victim of her own vanity, and against that, against the belief in her own fascinations, against the very part of herself that gives all the colour to her life, who shall expect a woman to take up arms?'

'Are you so vain, Elizabeth?' inquired Irais with a shocked face, 'and had you lent a willing ear to the blandishments of ninety-nine before you reached your final destiny?'

'I am one of the sensible ones, I suppose,' I replied, 'for nobody ever wanted me to listen to blandishments.'

Minora sighed.

'I like to hear you talk together about the position of women,' he went on, 'and wonder when you will realise that they hold exactly the position they are fitted for. As soon as they are fit to occupy a better, no power on earth will be able to keep them out of it. Meanwhile, let me warn you that, as things now are, only strong-minded women wish to see you the equals of men, and the strong-minded are invariably plain. The pretty ones would rather see men their slaves than their equals.'

'You know,' said Irais, frowning, 'that I consider myself strong-minded.'

'And never rise till lunch-time?'

Irais blushed. Although I don't approve of such conduct, it is very convenient in more ways than one; I get through my house-keeping undisturbed, and whenever she is disposed to lecture me, I begin about this habit of hers. Her conscience must be terribly stricken on the point, for she is by no means as a rule given to meekness.

'A woman without vanity would be unattackable,' resumed the Man of Wrath. 'When a girl enters that downward path that leads to ruin, she is led solely by her own vanity; for in these days of policemen no young woman can be forced against her will from the path of virtue, and the cries of the injured are never heard until the destroyer begins to express his penitence for having destroyed. If his passion could remain at white-heat and he could continue to feed her ear with the protestations she loves, no principles of piety or virtue would disturb the happiness of his companion; for a mournful experience teaches that piety begins only where passion ends, and that principles are strongest where temptations are most rare.'

'But what has all this to do with us?' I inquired severely.

'You were displeased at our law classing you as it does, and I merely wish to justify it,' he answered. 'Creatures who habitually say yes to everything a man proposes, when no one can oblige them to say it, and when it is so often fatal, are plainly not responsible beings.'

'I shall never say it to you again, my dear man,' I said.

'And not only that fatal weakness,' he continued, 'but what is there, candidly, to distinguish you from children? You are older, but not wiser, — really not so wise, for with years you lose the common sense you had as children. Have you ever heard a group of women talking reasonably together?'

'Yes — we do!' Irais and I cried in a breath.

'It has interested me,' went on the Man of Wrath, 'in my idle moments, to listen to their talk. It amused me to hear the malicious little stories they told of their best friends who were absent, to note the spiteful little digs they gave their best friends who were present, to watch the utter incredulity with which they listened to the tale of some other woman's conquests, the radiant good faith they displayed in connection with their own, the instant collapse into boredom, if some topic of so-called general interest, by some extraordinary chance, were introduced.' 'You must have belonged to a particularly nice set,' remarked Irais.

'And as for politics,' he said, 'I have never heard them mentioned among women.'

'Children and idiots are not interested in such things,' I said.

'And we are much too frightened of being put in prison,' said Irais.

'In prison?' echoed Minora.

'Don't you know,' said Irais, turning to her 'that if you talk about such things here you run a great risk of being imprisoned?'

'But why?'

'But why? Because, though you yourself may have meant nothing but what was innocent, your words may have suggested something less innocent to the evil minds of your hearers; and then the law steps in, and calls it dolus eventualis, and everybody says how dreadful, and off you go to prison and are punished as you deserve to be.'

Minora looked mystified.

'That is not, however, your real reason for not discussing them,' said the Man of Wrath; 'they simply do not interest you. Or it may be, that you do not consider your female friends' opinions worth listening to, for you certainly display an astonishing thirst for information when male politicians are present. I have seen a pretty young woman, hardly in her twenties, sitting a whole evening drinking in the doubtful wisdom of an elderly political star, with every appearance of eager interest. He was a bimetallic star, and was giving her whole pamphletsful of information.'

'She wanted to make up to him for some reason,' said Irais, 'and got him to explain his hobby to her, and he was silly enough to be taken in. Now which was the sillier in that case?'

She threw herself back in her chair and looked up defiantly, beating her foot impatiently on the carpet.

'She wanted to be thought clever,' said the Man of Wrath. 'What puzzled me,' he went on musingly, 'was that she went away apparently as serene and happy as when she came. The explanation of the principles of bimetallism produce, as a rule, a contrary effect.'

'Why, she hadn't been listening,' cried Irais, 'and your simple star had been making a fine goose of himself the whole evening.

'Prattle, prattle, simple star,
Bimetallic, wunderbar.
Though you're given to describe
Woman as a dummes Weib.
You yourself are sillier far,
Prattling, bimetallic star!'

'No doubt she had understood very little,' said the Man of Wrath, taking no notice of this effusion.

'And no doubt the gentleman hadn't understood much either.' Irais was plainly irritated.

'Your opinion of woman,' said Minora in a very small voice, 'is not a high one. But, in the sick chamber, I suppose you agree that no one could take her place?'

'If you are thinking of hospital-nurses,' I said, 'I must tell you that I believe he married chiefly that he might have a wife instead of a strange woman to nurse him when he is sick.'

'But,' said Minora, bewildered at the way her illusions were being knocked about, 'the sick-room is surely the very place of all others in which a woman's gentleness and tact are most valuable.'

'Gentleness and tact?' repeated the Man of Wrath. 'I have never met those qualities in the professional nurse. According to my experience, she is a disagreeable person who finds in private nursing exquisite opportunities for asserting her superiority over ordinary and prostrate mankind. I know of no more humiliating position for a man than to be in bed having his feverish brow soothed by a sprucely-dressed strange woman, bristling with starch and spotlessness. He would give half his income for his clothes, and probably the other half if she would leave him alone, and go away altogether. He feels her superiority through every pore; he never before realised how absolutely inferior he is; he is abjectly polite, and contemptibly conciliatory; if a friend comes to see him, he eagerly praises her in case she should be listening behind the screen; he cannot call his soul his own, and, what is far more intolerable, neither is he sure that his body really belongs to him; he has read of ministering angels and the light touch of a woman's hand, but the day on which he can ring for his servant and put on his socks in private fills him with the same sort of wildness of joy that he felt as a homesick schoolboy at the end of his first term.'

Minora was silent. Irais's foot was livelier than ever. The Man of Wrath stood smiling

162

blandly down upon us. You can't argue with a person so utterly convinced of his infallibility that he won't even get angry with you; so we sat round and said nothing.

'If,' he went on, addressing Irais, who looked rebellious, 'you doubt the truth of my remarks, and still cling to the old poetic notion of noble, self-sacrificing women tenderly helping the patient over the rough places on the road to death or recovery, let me beg you to try for yourself, next time any one in your house is ill, whether the actual fact in any way corresponds to the picturesque belief. The angel who is to alleviate our sufferings comes in such a questionable shape, that to the unimaginative she appears merely as an extremely self-confident young woman, wisely concerned first of all in securing her personal comfort, much given to complaints about her food and to helplessness where she should be helpful, possessing an extraordinary capacity for fancying herself slighted, or not regarded as the superior being she knows herself to be, morbidly anxious lest the servants should, by some mistake, treat her with offensive cordiality, pettish if the patient gives more trouble than she had expected, intensely injured and disagreeable if he is made so courageous by his wretchedness as to wake her during the night — an act of desperation of which I was guilty once, and once only. Oh, these good women! What sane man wants to have to do with angels? And especially do we object to having them about us when we are sick and sorry, when we feel in every fibre what poor things we are, and when all our fortitude is needed to enable us to bear our temporary inferiority patiently, without being forced besides to assume an attitude of eager and grovelling politeness towards the angel in the house.'

There was a pause.

'I didn't know you could talk so much, Sage,' said Irais at length.

'What would you have women do, then?' asked Minora meekly. Irais began to beat her foot up and down again, — what did it matter what Men of Wrath would have us do? 'There are not,' continued Minora, blushing, 'husbands enough for every one, and the rest must do something.'

'Certainly,' replied the oracle. 'Study the art of pleasing by dress and manner as long as you are of an age to interest us, and above all, let all women, pretty and plain, married and single, study the art of cookery. If you are an artist in the kitchen you will always be esteemed.'

I sat very still. Every German woman, even the wayward Irais, has learned to cook; I seem to have been the only one who was naughty and wouldn't.

'Only be careful,' he went on, 'in studying both arts, never to forget the great truth that dinner precedes blandishments and not blandishments dinner. A man must be made comfortable before he will make love to you; and though it is true that if you offered him a choice between Spickgans and kisses, he would say he would take both, yet he would invariably begin with the Spickgans, and allow the kisses to wait.'

At this I got up, and Irais followed my example. 'Your cynicism is disgusting,' I said icily.

'You two are always exceptions to anything I may say,' he said, smiling amiably.

He stooped and kissed Irais's hand. She is inordinately vain of her hands, and says her husband married her for their sake, which I can quite believe. I am glad they are on her and not on Minora, for if Minora had had them I should have been annoyed. Minora's are bony, with chilly-looking knuckles, ignored nails, and too much wrist. I feel very well disposed towards her when my eye falls on them. She put one forward now, evidently thinking it would be kissed too.

'Did you know,' said Irais, seeing the movement, 'that it is the custom here to kiss women's hands?'

'But only married women's,' I added, not desiring her to feel out of it, 'never young girls'.'

She drew it in again. 'It is a pretty custom,' she said with a sigh; and pensively inscribed it in her book.

* * *

January 15th. — The bills for my roses and bulbs and other last year's horticultural indulgences were all on the table when I came down to breakfast this morning. They rather frightened me. Gardening is expensive, I find, when it has to be paid for out of one's own private pin-money. The Man of Wrath does not in the least want roses, or flowering shrubs, or plantations, or new paths, and therefore, he asks, why should he pay for them? So he does not and I do, and I have to make up for it by not indulging all too riotously in new clothes, which is no doubt very chastening. I certainly prefer buying new rose-trees to new dresses, if I cannot comfortably have both; and I see a time coming when the passion for my garden will have taken such a hold on me that I shall not only entirely cease buying more clothes, but begin to sell those that I already have. The garden is so big that everything has to be bought wholesale; and I fear I shall not be able to go on much longer with only one man and a stork, because the more I plant the more there will be to water in the inevitable drought, and the watering is a serious consideration when it means going backwards and forwards all day long to a pump near the house, with a little water-cart. People living in England, in almost perpetual mildness and moisture, don't really know what a drought is. If they have some weeks of cloudless weather, it is generally preceded and followed by good rains; but we have perhaps an hour's shower every week, and then comes a month or six weeks' drought. The soil is very light, and dries so quickly that, after the heaviest thunder-shower, I can walk over any of my paths in my thin shoes; and to keep the garden even moderately damp it should pour with rain regularly every day for three hours. My only means of getting water is to go to the pump near the house, or to the little stream that forms my eastern boundary, and the little stream dries up too unless there has been rain, and is at the best of times difficult to get at, having steep banks covered with forget-me-nots. I possess one moist, peaty bit of ground, and that is to be planted with silver birches in imitation of the Hirschwald, and is to be carpeted between the birches with flaming azaleas. All the rest of my soil is sandy — the soil for pines and acacias, but not the soil for roses; yet see what love will do — there are more roses in my garden than any other flower! Next spring the bare places are to be filled with trees that I have ordered: pines behind the delicate acacias, and startling mountain-ashes, oaks, copper-beeches, maples, larches, juniper-trees — was it not Elijah who sat down to rest under a juniper-tree? I have often wondered how he managed to get under it. It is a compact little tree, not more than two to three yards high here, and all closely squeezed up together. Perhaps they grew more aggressively where he was. By the time the babies have grown old and disagreeable it will be very pretty here, and then possibly they won't like it; and, if they have inherited the Man of Wrath's indifference to gardens, they will let it run wild and leave it to return to the state in which I found it. Or perhaps their three husbands will refuse to live in it, or to come to such a lonely place at all, and then of course its fate is sealed. My only comfort is that husbands don't flourish in the desert, and that the three will have to wait a long time before enough are found to go round. Mothers tell me that it is a dreadful business finding one husband; how much more painful then to have to look for three at once! — the babies are so nearly the same age that they only just escaped being twins. But I won't look. I can imagine nothing more uncomfortable than a son-in-law, and besides, I don't think a husband is at all a good thing for a girl to have. I shall do my best in the years at my disposal to train them so to love the garden, and outdoor life, and even farming, that, if they have a spark of their mother in them, they will want and ask for nothing better. My hope of success is however exceedingly small, and there is probably a fearful period in store for me when I shall be taken every day during the winter to the distant towns to balls — a poor old mother shivering in broad daylight in her party gown, and being made to start after an early lunch and not getting home till breakfasttime next morning. Indeed, they have already developed an alarming desire to go to 'partings' as they call them, the April baby announcing her intention of beginning to do so when she is twelve. 'Are you twelve, Mummy?' she asked.

The gardener is leaving on the first of April, and I am trying to find another. It is grievous changing so often — in two years I shall have had three — because at each change a great part of my plants and plans necessarily suffers. Seeds get lost, seedlings are not pricked out in time, places already sown are planted with something else, and there is confusion out of doors and despair in my heart. But he was to have married the cook, and the cook saw a ghost and immediately left, and he is going after her as soon as he can, and meanwhile is wasting visibly away. What she saw was doors that are locked opening with a great clatter all by themselves on the hingeside, and then somebody invisible cursed at her. These phenomena now go by the name of 'the ghost.' She asked to be allowed to leave at once, as she had never been in a place where there was a ghost before. I suggested that she should try and get used to it; but she thought it would be wasting time, and she looked so ill that I let her go, and the garden has to suffer. I don't know why it should be given to cooks to see such interesting things and withheld from me, but I have had two others since she left, and they both have seen the ghost. Minora grows very silent as bed-time approaches, and relents towards Irais and myself; and, after having shown us all day how little she approves us, when the bedroom candles are brought she quite begins to cling. She has once or twice anxiously inquired whether Irais is sure she does not object to sleeping alone.

'If you are at all nervous, I will come and

keep you company,' she said; 'I don't mind at all, I assure you.'

But Irais is not to be taken in by such simple wiles, and has told me she would rather sleep with fifty ghosts than with one Minora.

Since Miss Jones was so unexpectedly called away to her parent's bedside I have seen a good deal of the babies; and it is so nice without a governess that I would put off engaging another for a year or two, if it were not that I should in so doing come within the reach of the arm of the law, which is what every German spends his life in trying to avoid. The April baby will be six next month, and, after her sixth birthday is passed, we are liable at any moment to receive a visit from a school inspector, who will inquire curiously into the state of her education, and, if it is not up to the required standard, all sorts of fearful things might happen to the guilty parents, probably beginning with fines, and going on crescendo to dungeons if, owing to gaps between governesses and difficulties in finding the right one, we persisted in our evil courses. Shades of the prison-house begin to close here upon the growing boy, and prisons compass the Teuton about on every side all through life to such an extent that he has to walk very delicately indeed if he would stay outside them and pay for their maintenance.

Cultured individuals do not, as a rule, neglect to teach their offspring to read, and write, and say their prayers, and are apt to resent the intrusion of an examining inspector into their homes; but it does not much matter after all, and I daresay it is very good for us to be worried; indeed, a philosopher of my acquaintance declares that people who are not regularly and properly worried are never any good for anything. In the eye of the law we are all sinners, and every man is held to be guilty until he has proved that he is innocent.

Minora has seen so much of the babies that, after vainly trying to get out of their way for several days, she thought it better to resign herself, and make the best of it by regarding them as copy, and using them to fill a chapter in her book. So she took to dogging their footsteps wherever they went, attended their uprisings and their lyings down, engaged them, if she could, in intelligent conversation, went with them into the garden to study their ways when they were sleighing, drawn by a big dog, and generally made their lives a burden to them. This went on for three days, and then she settled down to write the result with the Man of Wrath's typewriter, borrowed whenever her notes for any chapter have reached the state of ripeness necessary for the process she describes as 'throwing into form.' She writes everything with a typewriter, even her private letters.

'Don't forget to put in something about a mother's knee,' said Irais; 'you can't write effectively about children without that.'

'Oh, of course I shall mention that,' replied Minora.

'And pink toes,' I added. 'There are always toes, and they are never anything but pink.'

'I have that somewhere,' said Minora, turning over her notes.

'But, after all, babies are not a German speciality,' said Irais, 'and I don't quite see why you should bring them into a book of German travels. Elizabeth's babies have each got the fashionable number of arms and legs, and are exactly the same as English ones.'

'Oh, but they can't be just the same, you know,' said Minora, looking worried. 'It must make a difference living here in this place, and eating such odd things, and never having a doctor, and never being ill. Children who have never had measles and those things can't be quite the same as other children; it must all be in their systems and can't get out for some reason or other. And a child brought up on chicken and rice-pudding must be different to a child that eats Spickgans and liver sausages. And they are different; I can't tell in what way, but they certainly are; and I think if I steadily describe them from the materials I have collected the last three days, I may perhaps hit on the points of difference.'

'Why bother about points of difference?' asked Irais. 'I should write some little thing, bringing in the usual parts of the picture, such as knees and toes, and make it mildly pathetic.'

'But it is by no means an easy thing for me to do,' said Minora plaintively; 'I have so little experience of children.'

'Then why write it at all?' asked that sensible person Elizabeth.

'I have as little experience as you,' said Irais, 'because I have no children; but if you don't yearn after startling originality, nothing is easier than to write bits about them. I believe I could do a dozen in an hour.'

She sat down at the writing-table, took up an old letter, and scribbled for about five minutes. 'There,' she said, throwing it to Minora, 'you may have it — pink toes and all complete.'

Minora put on her eye-glasses and read aloud:

'When my baby shuts her eyes and sings her hymns at bed-time my stale and battered soul is filled with awe. All sorts of vague memories crowd into my mind — memories of my own mother and myself — how many years ago! — of the sweet helplessness of being gathered up half asleep in her arms, and undressed, and put in my cot, without being wakened; of the angels I believed in; of little children coming straight from heaven, and still being surrounded, so long as they were good, by the shadow of white wings, — all the dear poetic nonsense learned, just as my baby is learning it, at her mother's knee. She has not an idea of the beauty of the charming things she is told, and stares wide-eyed, with heavenly eyes, while her mother talks of the heaven she has so lately come from, and is relieved and comforted by the interrupting bread and milk. At two years old she does not understand angels, and does understand bread and milk; at five she has vague notions about them, and prefers bread and milk; at ten both bread and milk and angels have been left behind in the nursery, and she has already found out that they are luxuries not necessary to her everyday life. In later years she may be disinclined to accept truths second-hand, insist on thinking for herself, be earnest in her desire to shake off exploded traditions, be untiring in her efforts to live according to a high moral standard and to be strong, and pure, and good — '

'Like tea,' explained Irais.

' — yet will she never, with all her virtues, possess one-thousandth part of the charm that clung about her when she sang, with quiet eyelids, her first reluctant hymns, kneeling on her mother's knees. I love to come in at bed-time and sit in the window in the setting sunshine watching the mysteries of her going to bed. Her mother tubs her, for she is far too precious to be touched by any nurse, and then she is rolled up in a big bath towel, and only her little pink toes peep out; and when she is powdered, and combed, and tied up in her night-dress, and all her curls are on end, and her ears glowing, she is knelt down on her mother's lap, a little bundle of fragrant flesh, and her face reflects the quiet of her mother's face as she goes through her evening prayer for pity and for peace.'

'How very curious!' said Minora, when she had finished. 'That is exactly what I was going to say.'

'Oh, then I have saved you the trouble of putting it together; you can copy that if you like.'

'But have you a stale soul, Miss Minora?' I asked.

'Well, do you know, I rather think that is a good touch,' she replied; 'it will make people really think a man wrote the book. You know I am going to take a man's name.'

'That is precisely what I imagined,' said Irais. 'You will call yourself John Jones, or George Potts, or some such sternly commonplace name, to emphasise your uncompromising attitude towards all feminine weaknesses, and no one will be taken in.'

'I really think, Elizabeth,' said Irais to me later, when the click of Minora's typewriter was heard hesitating in the next room, 'that you and I are writing her book for her. She takes down everything we say. Why does she copy all that about the baby? I wonder why mothers' knees are supposed to be touching? I never learned anything at them, did you? But then in my case they were only stepmother's, and nobody ever sings their praises.'

'My mother was always at parties,' I said; 'and the nurse made me say my prayers in French.'

'And as for tubs and powder,' went on Irais, 'when I was a baby such things were not the fashion. There were never any bathrooms, and no tubs; our faces and hands were washed, and there was a foot-bath in the room, and in the summer we had a bath and were put to bed afterwards for fear we might catch cold. My stepmother didn't worry much; she used to wear pink dresses all over lace, and the older she got the prettier the dresses got. When is she going?'

'Who? Minora? I haven't asked her that.'

'Then I will. It is really bad for her art to be neglected like this. She has been here an unconscionable time, — it must be nearly three weeks.'

'Yes, she came the same day you did,' I said pleasantly.

Irais was silent. I hope she was reflecting that it is not worse to neglect one's art than one's husband, and her husband is lying all this time stretched on a bed of sickness, while she is spending her days so agreeably with me. She has a way of forgetting that she has a home, or any other business in the world than just to stay on chatting with me, and reading, and singing, and laughing at any one there is to laugh at, and kissing the babies, and tilting with the Man of Wrath. Naturally I love her — she is so pretty that anybody with eyes in his head must love her — but too much of anything is bad, and next month the passages and offices are to be whitewashed, and people who have ever whitewashed their houses inside know what nice places they are to live in while it is being done; and there will be no dinner for Irais, and none of those succulent salads full of caraway seeds that she so devotedly loves. I shall begin to lead her thoughts gently back to her duties by inquiring every day anxiously after her husband's health. She is not very fond of him, because he does not run and hold the door open for her every time she gets up to leave the room; and though she has asked him to do so, and told him how much she wishes he would, he still won't. She stayed once in a house where there was an Englishman, and his nimbleness in regard to doors and chairs so impressed her that her husband has had no peace since, and each time she has to go out of a room she is reminded of her disregarded wishes, so that a shut door is to her symbolic of the failure of her married life, and the very sight of one makes her wonder why she was born; at least, that is what she told me once, in a burst of confidence. He is quite a nice, harmless little man, pleasant to talk to, good-tempered, and full of fun; but he thinks he is too old to begin to learn new and uncomfortable ways, and he has that horror of being made better by his wife that distinguishes so many righteous men, and is shared by the Man of Wrath, who persists in holding his glass in his left hand at meals, because if he did not (and I don't believe he particularly likes doing it) his relations might say that marriage has improved him, and thus drive the iron into his soul. This habit occasions an almost daily argument between one or other of the babies and myself.

'April, hold your glass in your right hand.'

'But papa doesn't.'

'When you are as old as papa you can do as you like.'

Which was embellished only yesterday by Minora adding impressively, 'And only think how strange it would look if everybody held their glasses so.'

April was greatly struck by the force of this proposition.

★   ★   ★

January 28th. — It is very cold, — fifteen degrees of frost Reaumur, but perfectly delicious, still, bright weather, and one feels jolly and energetic and amiably disposed towards everybody. The two young ladies are still here, but the air is so buoyant that even they don't weigh on me any longer, and besides, they have both announced their approaching departure, so that after all I shall get my whitewashing done in peace, and the house will have on its clean pinafore in time to welcome the spring.

Minora has painted my portrait, and is going to present it as a parting gift to the Man of Wrath; and the fact that I let her do it, and sat meekly times innumerable, proves conclusively, I hope, that I am not vain. When Irais first saw it she laughed till she cried, and at once commissioned her to paint hers, so that she may take it away with her and give it to her husband on his birthday, which happens to be early in February. Indeed, if it were not for this birthday, I really think she would have forgotten to go at all; but birthdays are great and solemn festivals with us, never allowed to slip by unnoticed, and always celebrated in the presence of a sympathetic crowd of relations (gathered from far and near to tell you how well you are wearing, and that nobody would ever dream, and that really it is wonderful), who stand round a sort of sacrificial altar, on which your years are offered up as a burnt-offering to the gods in the shape of lighted pink and white candles, stuck in a very large, flat, jammy cake. The cake with its candles is the chief feature, and on the table round it lie the gifts each person present is more or less bound to give. As my birthday falls in the winter I get mittens as well as blotting-books and photograph-frames, and if it were in the summer I should get photograph-frames and blotting-books and no mittens; but whatever the present may be, and by whomsoever given, it has to be welcomed with the noisiest gratitude, and loudest exclamations of joy, and such words as entzuckend, reizend, herrlich, wundervoll, and suss repeated over and over again, until the unfortunate Geburtstagskind feels indeed that another year has gone, and that she has grown older, and wiser, and more tired of folly and of vain repetitions. A flag is hoisted, and all the morning the rites are celebrated, the cake eaten, healths drunk, speeches made, and hands nearly shaken off. The neighbouring parsons drive up, and when nobody is looking their wives count the candles in the cake; the active lady in the next Schlass spares time to send a pot of flowers, and to look up my age in the Gotha Almanach; a deputation comes from the farms headed by the chief inspector in white kid gloves who invokes Heaven's blessings on the gracious lady's head; and the babies are enchanted, and sit in a corner trying on all the mittens. In the evening there is a dinner for the relations and the chief local authorities, with more health-drinking and speechifying, and the next morning, when I come downstairs thankful to have done with it, I am confronted by the altar still in its place, cake crumbs and candle-grease and all, because any hasty removal of it would imply a most lamentable want of sentiment, deplorable in anybody, but scandalous and disgusting in a tender female. All birthdays are observed in this fashion, and not a few wise persons go for a short trip just about the time theirs is due, and I think I shall imitate them next year; only trips to the country or seaside in December are not usually pleasant, and if I go to a town there are sure to be relations in it, and then the cake will spring up mushroom-like from the teeming soil of their affection.

I hope it has been made evident in these pages how superior Irais and myself are to the ordinary weaknesses of mankind; if any further proof were needed, it is furnished by the fact that we both, in defiance of tradition, scorn this celebration of birthday rites. Years ago, when first I knew her, and long before we were either of us married, I sent her a little brass candlestick on her birthday; and when mine followed a few months later, she sent me a note-book. No notes were written in it, and on her next birthday I presented it to her; she thanked me profusely in the customary manner, and when my turn came I received the brass candlestick. Since then we alternately enjoy the possession of each of these articles, and the present question is comfortably settled once and for all, at a minimum of trouble and expense. We never mention this little arrangement except at the proper time, when we send a letter of fervid thanks.

This radiant weather, when mere living is a joy, and sitting still over the fire out of the question, has been going on for more than a week. Sleighing and skating have been our chief occupation, especially skating, which is more than usually fascinating here, because the place is intersected by small canals communicating with a lake and the river belonging to the lake, and as everything is frozen black and hard, we can skate for miles straight ahead without being obliged to turn round and come back again, — at all times an annoying, and even mortifying, proceeding. Irais skates beautifully: modesty is the only obstacle to my saying the same of myself; but I may remark that all Germans skate well, for the simple reason that every year of their lives, for three or four months, they may do it as much as they like. Minora was astonished and disconcerted by finding herself left behind, and arriving at the place where tea meets us half an hour after we had finished. In some places the banks of the canals are so high that only our heads appear level with the fields, and it is, as Minora noted in her book, a curious sight to see three female heads skimming along apparently by themselves, and enjoying it tremendously. When the banks are low, we appear to be gliding deliciously over the roughest ploughed fields, with or without legs according to circumstances. Before we start, I fix on the place

184

where tea and a sleigh are to meet us, and we drive home again; because skating against the wind is as detestable as skating with it is delightful, and an unkind Nature arranges its blowing without the smallest regard for our convenience. Yesterday, by way of a change, we went for a picnic to the shores of the Baltic, ice-bound at this season, and utterly desolate at our nearest point. I have a weakness for picnics, especially in winter, when the mosquitoes cease from troubling and the ant-hills are at rest; and of all my many favourite picnic spots this one on the Baltic is the loveliest and best. As it is a three-hours' drive, the Man of Wrath is loud in his lamentations when the special sort of weather comes which means, as experience has taught him, this particular excursion. There must be deep snow, hard frost, no wind, and a cloudless sky; and when, on waking up, I see these conditions fulfilled, then it would need some very potent reason to keep me from having out a sleigh and going off. It is, I admit, a hard day for the horses; but why have horses if they are not to take you where you want to go to, and at the time you want to go? And why should not horses have hard days as well as everybody else? The Man of Wrath loathes picnics, and has no eye for nature and frozen seas, and is

185

simply bored by a long drive through a forest that does not belong to him; a single turnip on his own place is more admirable in his eyes than the tallest, pinkest, straightest pine that ever reared its snow-crowned head against the setting sunlight. Now observe the superiority of woman, who sees that both are good, and after having gazed at the pine and been made happy by its beauty, goes home and placidly eats the turnip. He went once and only once to this particular place, and made us feel so small by his blast behaviour that I never invite him now. It is a beautiful spot, endless forest stretching along the shore as far as the eye can reach; and after driving through it for miles you come suddenly, at the end of an avenue of arching trees, upon the glistening, oily sea, with the orange-coloured sails of distant fishing-smacks shilling in the sunlight. Whenever I have been there it has been windless weather, and the silence so profound that I could hear my pulses beating. The humming of insects and the sudden scream of a jay are the only sounds in summer, and in winter the stillness is the stillness of death.

Every paradise has its serpent, however, and this one is so infested by mosquitoes during the season when picnics seem most natural, that those of my visitors who have been taken there for a treat have invariably lost their tempers, and made the quiet shores ring with their wailing and lamentations. These despicable but irritating insects don't seem to have anything to do but to sit in multitudes on the sand, waiting for any prey Providence may send them; and as soon as the carriage appears they rise up in a cloud, and rush to meet us, almost dragging us out bodily, and never leave us until we drive away again. The sudden view of the sea from the messy, pine-covered height directly above it where we picnic; the wonderful stretch of lonely shore with the forest to the water's edge; the coloured sails in the blue distance; the freshness, the brightness, the vastness — all is lost upon the picnickers, and made worse than indifferent to them, by the perpetual necessity they are under of fighting these horrid creatures. It is nice being the only person who ever goes there or shows it to anybody, but if more people went, perhaps the mosquitoes would be less lean, and hungry, and pleased to see us. It has, however, the advantage of being a suitable place to which to take refractory visitors when they have stayed too long, or left my books out in the garden all night, or otherwise made their presence a burden too grievous to be borne; then one fine hot morning when they are all looking limp, I suddenly propose a picnic on the Baltic. I have never known this proposal fail to be greeted with exclamations of surprise and delight.

'The Baltic! You never told us you were within driving distance? How heavenly to get a breath of sea air on a day like this! The very thought puts new life into one! And how delightful to see the Baltic! Oh, please take us!' And then I take them.

But on a brilliant winter's day my conscience is as clear as the frosty air itself, and yesterday morning we started off in the gayest of spirits, even Minora being disposed to laugh immoderately on the least provocation. Only our eyes were allowed to peep out from the fur and woollen wrappings necessary to our heads if we would come back with our ears and noses in the same places they were in when we started, and for the first two miles the mirth created by each other's strange appearance was uproarious, — a fact I mention merely to show what an effect dry, bright, intense cold produces on healthy bodies, and how much better it is to go out in it and enjoy it than to stay indoors and sulk. As we passed through the neighbouring village with cracking of whip and jingling of bells, heads popped up at the windows to stare, and the only living thing in the silent, sunny street was a melancholy fowl with ruffled feathers, which looked at us reproachfully, as we dashed with so much energy over the crackling snow.

'Oh, foolish bird!' Irais called out as we passed; 'you'll be indeed a cold fowl if you stand there motionless, and every one prefers them hot in weather like this!'

And then we all laughed exceedingly, as though the most splendid joke had been made, and before we had done we were out of the village and in the open country beyond, and could see my house and garden far away behind, glittering in the sunshine; and in front of us lay the forest, with its vistas of pines stretching away into infinity, and a drive through it of fourteen miles before we reached the sea. It was a hoar-frost day, and the forest was an enchanted forest leading into fairyland, and though Irais and I have been there often before, and always thought it beautiful, yet yesterday we stood under the final arch of frosted trees, struck silent by the sheer loveliness of the place. For a long way out the sea was frozen, and then there was a deep blue line, and a cluster of motionless orange sails; at our feet a narrow strip of pale yellow sand; right and left the line of sparkling forest; and we ourselves standing in a world of white and diamond traceries. The stillness of an eternal Sunday lay on the place like a benediction.

Minora broke the silence by remarking that Dresden was pretty, but she thought this beat it almost.

'I don't quite see,' said Irais in a hushed voice, as though she were in a holy place, 'how the two can be compared.'

'Yes, Dresden is more convenient, of course,' replied Minora; after which we turned away and thought we would keep her quiet by feeding her, so we went back to the sleigh and had the horses taken out and their cloths put on, and they were walked up and down a distant glade while we sat in the sleigh and picnicked. It is a hard day for the horses, — nearly thirty miles there and back and no stable in the middle; but they are so fat and spoiled that it cannot do them much harm sometimes to taste the bitterness of life. I warmed soup in a little apparatus I have for such occasions, which helped to take the chilliness off the sandwiches, — this is the only unpleasant part of a winter picnic, the clammy quality of the provisions just when you most long for something very hot. Minora let her nose very carefully out of its wrappings, took a mouthful, and covered it up quickly again. She was nervous lest it should be frost-nipped, and truth compels me to add that her nose is not a bad nose, and might even be pretty on anybody else; but she does not know how to carry it, and there is an art in the angle at which one's nose is held just as in everything else, and really noses were intended for something besides mere blowing.

It is the most difficult thing in the world to eat sandwiches with immense fur and woollen gloves on, and I think we ate almost as much fur as anything, and choked exceedingly during the process. Minora was angry at this, and at last pulled off her glove, but quickly put it on again.

'How very unpleasant,' she remarked after swallowing a large piece of fur.

'It will wrap round your pipes, and keep them warm,' said Irais.

'Pipes!' echoed Minora, greatly disgusted by such vulgarity.

'I'm afraid I can't help you,' I said, as she continued to choke and splutter; 'we are all in the same case, and I don't know how to alter it.' 'There are such things as forks, I suppose,' snapped Minora.

'That's true,' said I, crushed by the obviousness of the remedy; but of what use are forks if they are fifteen miles off? So Minora had to continue to eat her gloves.

By the time we had finished, the sun was

already low behind the trees and the clouds beginning to flush a faint pink. The old coachman was given sandwiches and soup, and while he led the horses up and down with one hand and held his lunch in the other, we packed up — or, to be correct, I packed, and the others looked on and gave me valuable advice.

This coachman, Peter by name, is seventy years old, and was born on the place, and has driven its occupants for fifty years, and I am nearly as fond of him as I am of the sun-dial; indeed, I don't know what I should do without him, so entirely does he appear to understand and approve of my tastes and wishes. No drive is too long or difficult for the horses if I want to take it, no place impossible to reach if I want to go to it, no weather or roads too bad to prevent my going out if I wish to: to all my suggestions he responds with the readiest cheerfulness, and smoothes away all objections raised by the Man of Wrath, who rewards his alacrity in doing my pleasure by speaking of him as an alter Esel. In the summer, on fine evenings, I love to drive late and alone in the scented forests, and when I have reached a dark part stop, and sit quite still, listening to the nightingales repeating their little tune over and over again after interludes of gurgling, or if there are no nightingales, listening to the marvellous silence, and letting its blessedness descend into my very soul. The nightingales in the forests about here all sing the same tune, and in the same key of (E flat).

I don't know whether all nightingales do this, or if it is peculiar to this particular spot. When they have sung it once, they clear their throats a little, and hesitate, and then do it again, and it is the prettiest little song in the world. How could I indulge my passion for these drives with their pauses without Peter? He is so used to them that he stops now at the right moment without having to be told, and he is ready to drive me all night if I wish it, with no sign of anything but cheerful willingness on his nice old face. The Man of Wrath deplores these eccentric tastes, as he calls them, of mine; but has given up trying to prevent my indulging them because, while he is deploring in one part of the house, I have slipped out at a door in the other, and am gone before he can catch me, and have reached and am lost in the shadows of the forest by the time he has discovered that I am nowhere to be found.

The brightness of Peter's perfections are sullied however by one spot, and that is, that as age creeps upon him, he not only cannot hold the horses in if they don't want to be held in, but he goes to sleep sometimes on his box if I have him out too soon after lunch, and has upset me twice within the last year — once last winter out of a sleigh, and once this summer, when the horses shied at a bicycle, and bolted into the ditch on one side of the chaussee (German for high road), and the bicycle was so terrified at the horses shying that it shied too into the ditch on the other side, and the carriage was smashed, and the bicycle was smashed, and we were all very unhappy, except Peter, who never lost his pleasant smile, and looked so placid that my tongue clave to the roof of my mouth when I tried to make it scold him.

'But I should think he ought to have been thoroughly scolded on an occasion like that,' said Minora, to whom I had been telling this story as we wandered on the yellow sands while the horses were being put in the sleigh; and she glanced nervously up at Peter, whose mild head was visible between the bushes above us. 'Shall we get home before dark?' she asked.

The sun had altogether disappeared behind the pines and only the very highest of the little clouds were still pink; out at sea the mists were creeping up, and the sails of the fishing-smacks had turned a dull brown; a flight of wild geese passed across the disc of the moon with loud cacklings.

'Before dark?' echoed Irais, 'I should think not. It is dark now nearly in the forest, and we shall have the loveliest moonlight drive back.'

'But it is surely very dangerous to let a man who goes to sleep drive you,' said Minora apprehensively.

'But he's such an old dear,' I said.

'Yes, yes, no doubt,' she replied tastily; 'but there are wakeful old dears to be had, and on a box they are preferable.'

Irais laughed. 'You are growing quite amusing, Miss Minora,' she said.

'He isn't on a box to-day,' said I; 'and I never knew him to go to sleep standing up behind us on a sleigh.' But Minora was not to be appeased, and muttered something about seeing no fun in foolhardiness, which shows how alarmed she was, for it was rude.

Peter, however, behaved beautifully on the way home, and Irais and I at least were as happy as possible driving back, with all the glories of the western sky flashing at us every now and then at the end of a long avenue as we swiftly passed, and later on, when they had faded, myriads of stars in the narrow black strip of sky over our heads. It was bitterly cold, and Minora was silent, and not in the least inclined to laugh with us as she had been six hours before.

'Have you enjoyed yourself, Miss Minora?' inquired Irais, as we got out of the forest on to the chaussee, and the lights of the village before ours twinkled in the distance.

'How many degrees do you suppose there are now?' was Minora's reply to this question.

'Degrees? — Of frost? Oh, dear me, are you cold,' cried Irais solicitously.

'Well, it isn't exactly warm, is it?' said Minora sulkily; and Irais pinched me. 'Well, but think how much colder you would have been without all that fur you ate for lunch inside you,' she said. 'And what a nice chapter you will be able to write about the Baltic,' said I. 'Why, it is practically certain that you are the first English person who has ever been to just this part of it.'

'Isn't there some English poem,' said Irais, 'about being the first who ever burst — '

' "Into that silent sea," ' finished Minora hastily. 'You can't quote that without its context, you know.'

'But I wasn't going to,' said Irais meekly; 'I only paused to breathe. I must breathe, or perhaps I might die.'

The lights from my energetic friend's Schloss shone brightly down upon us as we passed round the base of the hill on which it stands; she is very proud of this hill, as well she may be, seeing that it is the only one in

196

the whole district.

'Do you never go there?' asked Minora, jerking her head in the direction of the house.

'Sometimes. She is a very busy woman, and I should feel I was in the way if I went often.'

'It would be interesting to see another North German interior,' said Minora; 'and I should be obliged if you would take me.

'But I can't fall upon her suddenly with a strange girl,' I protested; 'and we are not at all on such intimate terms as to justify my taking all my visitors to see her.'

'What do you want to see another interior for?' asked Irais. 'I can tell you what it is like; and if you went nobody would speak to you, and if you were to ask questions, and began to take notes, the good lady would stare at you in the frankest amazement, and think Elizabeth had brought a young lunatic out for an airing. Everybody is not as patient as Elizabeth,' added Irais, anxious to pay off old scores.

'I would do a great deal for you, Miss Minora,' I said, 'but I can't do that.'

'If we went,' said Irais, 'Elizabeth and I would be placed with great ceremony on a sofa behind a large, polished oval table with a crochetmat in the centre — it has got a crochet-mat in the centre, hasn't it?' I nodded. 'And you would sit on one of the four little podgy, buttony, tasselly red chairs that are ranged on the other side of the table facing the sofa. They are red, Elizabeth?' Again I nodded. 'The floor is painted yellow, and there is no carpet except a rug in front of the sofa. The paper is dark chocolate colour, almost black; that is in order that after years of use the dirt may not show, and the room need not be done up. Dirt is like wickedness, you see, Miss Minora — its being there never matters; it is only when it shows so much as to be apparent to everybody that we are ashamed of it. At intervals round the high walls are chairs, and cabinets with lamps on them, and in one corner is a great white cold stove — or is it majolica?' she asked, turning to me.

'No, it is white.'

'There are a great many lovely big windows, all ready to let in the air and the sun, but they are as carefully covered with brown lace curtains under heavy stuff ones as though a whole row of houses were just opposite, with peering eyes at every window trying to look in, instead of there only being fields, and trees, and birds. No fire, no sunlight, no books, no flowers; but a consoling smell of red cabbage coming up under the door, mixed, in due season, with soapsuds.'

'When did you go there?' asked Minora.

'Ah, when did I go there indeed? When did

I not go there? I have been calling there all my life.'

Minora's eyes rolled doubtfully first at me then at Irais from the depths of her head-wrappings; they are large eyes with long dark eyelashes, and far be it from me to deny that each eye taken by itself is fine, but they are put in all wrong.

'The only thing you would learn there,' went on Irais, 'would be the significance of sofa corners in Germany. If we three went there together, I should be ushered into the right-hand corner of the sofa, because it is the place of honour, and I am the greatest stranger; Elizabeth would be invited to seat herself in the left-hand corner, as next in importance; the hostess would sit near us in an arm-chair; and you, as a person of no importance whatever, would either be left to sit where you could, or would be put on a chair facing us, and with the entire breadth of the table between us to mark the immense social gulf that separates the married woman from the mere virgin. These sofa corners make the drawing of nice distinctions possible in a way that nothing else could. The world might come to an end, and create less sensation in doing it, than you would, Miss Minora, if by any chance you got into the right-hand corner of one. That you are put on a chair on the other side of the table places you at once in the scale of precedence, and exactly defines your social position, or rather your complete want of a social position.' And Irais tilted her nose ever so little heavenwards.

'Note it,' she added, 'as the heading of your next chapter.'

'Note what?' asked Minora impatiently.

'Why, 'The Subtle Significance of Sofas', of course,' replied Irais. 'If,' she continued, as Minora made no reply appreciative of this suggestion, 'you were to call unexpectedly, the bad luck which pursues the innocent would most likely make you hit on a washing-day, and the distracted mistress of the house would keep you waiting in the cold room so long while she changed her dress, that you would begin to fear you were to be left to perish from want and hunger; and when she did appear, would show by the bitterness of her welcoming smile the rage that was boiling in her heart.'

'But what has the mistress of the house to do with washing?'

'What has she to do with washing? Oh, you sweet innocent — pardon my familiarity, but such ignorance of country-life customs is very touching in one who is writing a book about them.'

'Oh, I have no doubt I am very ignorant,'

said Minora loftily.

'Seasons of washing,' explained Irais, 'are seasons set apart by the Hausfrau to be kept holy. They only occur every two or three months, and while they are going on the whole house is in an uproar, every other consideration sacrificed, husband and children sunk into insignificance, and no one approaching, or interfering with the mistress of the house during these days of purification, but at their peril.'

'You Don't Really Mean,' Said Minora, 'that You Only Wash Your Clothes Four Times A Year?

'Yes, I do mean it,' replied Irais.

'Well, I think that is very disgusting,' said Minora emphatically.

Irais raised those pretty, delicate eyebrows of hers. 'Then you must take care and not marry a German,' she said.

'But what is the object of it?' went on Minora.

'Why, to clean the linen, I suppose.'

'Yes, yes, but why only at such long intervals?'

'It is an outward and visible sign of vast possessions in the shape of linen. If you were to want to have your clothes washed every week, as you do in England, you would be put down as a person who only has just enough to last that length of time, and would be an object of general contempt.'

'But I should be a clean object,' cried Minora, 'and my house would not be full of accumulated dirt.'

We said nothing — there was nothing to be said.

'It must be a happy land, that England of yours,' Irais remarked after a while with a sigh — a beatific vision no doubt presenting itself to her mind of a land full of washerwomen and agile gentlemen darting at door-handles.

'It is a clean land, at any rate,' replied Minora.

'I don't want to go and live in it,' I said — for we were driving up to the house, and a memory of fogs and umbrellas came into my mind as I looked up fondly at its dear old west front, and I felt that what I want is to live and die just here, and that there never was such a happy woman as Elizabeth.

★ ★ ★

April 18th. — I have been so busy ever since Irais and Minora left that I can hardly believe the spring is here, and the garden hurrying on its green and flowered petticoat — only its petticoat as yet, for though the underwood is a fairyland of tender little leaves, the trees above are still quite bare.

February was gone before I well knew that it had come, so deeply was I engaged in making hot-beds, and having them sown with petunias, verbenas, and nicotina affinis; while no less than thirty are dedicated solely to vegetables, it having been borne in upon me lately that vegetables must be interesting things to grow, besides possessing solid virtues not given to flowers, and that I might as well take the orchard and kitchen garden under my wing. So I have rushed in with all the zeal of utter inexperience, and my February evenings were spent poring over gardening books, and my days in applying the freshly absorbed wisdom. Who says that February is a dull, sad, slow month in the country? It was of the cheerfullest, swiftest description here, and its mild days enabled me to get on beautifully with the digging and manuring, and filled my rooms with snow-drops. The longer I live the greater is my respect and affection for manure in all its forms, and already, though the year is so young, a considerable portion of its pin-money has been spent on artificial manure. The Man of Wrath says he never met a young woman who spent her money that way before; I remarked that it must be nice to have an original wife; and he retorted that the word original hardly described me, and that the word eccentric was the one required. Very well, I suppose I am eccentric, since even my husband says so; but if my eccentricities are of such a practical nature as to result later in the biggest cauliflowers and tenderest lettuce in Prussia, why then he ought to be the first to rise up and call me blessed.

I sent to England for vegetable-marrow seeds, as they are not grown here, and people try and make boiled cucumbers take their place; but boiled cucumbers are nasty things, and I don't see why marrows should not do here perfectly well. These, and primrose-roots, are the English contributions to my garden. I brought over the roots in a tin box last time I came from England, and am anxious to see whether they will consent to live here. Certain it is that they don't exist in the Fatherland, so I can only conclude the winter kills them, for surely, if such lovely things would grow, they never would have been overlooked. Irais is deeply interested in the experiment; she reads so many English books, and has heard so much about primroses, and they have got so mixed up in her mind with leagues, and dames, and Disraelis, that she longs to see this mysterious political flower, and has made me promise to telegraph when it appears, and she will come over. But they are not going to do anything this year, and I only hope those cold days did not send them off to the Paradise of flowers. I am afraid their first impression of Germany was a chilly one.

Irais writes about once a week, and inquires after the garden and the babies, and announces her intention of coming back as soon as the numerous relations staying with her have left, — 'which they won't do,' she wrote the other day, 'until the first frosts nip them off, when they will disappear like belated dahlias — double ones of course, for single dahlias are too charming to be compared to relations. I have every sort of cousin and uncle and aunt here, and here they have been ever since my husband's birthday — not the same ones exactly, but I get so confused that I never know where one ends and the other begins. My husband goes off after breakfast to look at his crops, he says, and I am left at their mercy. I wish I had crops to go and look at — I should be grateful even for one, and would look at it from morning till night, and quite stare it out of countenance, sooner than stay at home and have the truth told me by enigmatic aunts. Do you know my Aunt Bertha? she, in particular, spends her time propounding obscure questions for my solution. I get so tired and worried trying to guess the answers, which are always truths supposed to be good for me to hear. 'Why do you wear your hair on your forehead?' she asks, — and that sets me off wondering why I do wear it on my forehead, and what she wants to know for, or whether she does know and only wants to know if I will answer truthfully. 'I am sure I don't know, aunt,' I say meekly, after puzzling over it for ever so long; 'perhaps my maid knows. Shall I ring and ask her?' And then she informs me that I wear it so to hide an ugly line she says I have down the middle of my forehead, and that betokens a listless and discontented disposition. Well, if she knew, what did she ask me for? Whenever I am with them they ask me riddles like that, and I simply lead a dog's life. Oh, my dear, relations are like drugs, — useful sometimes, and even pleasant, if taken in small quantities and seldom, but dreadfully pernicious on the whole, and the truly wise avoid them.'

From Minora I have only had one communication since her departure, in which she thanked me for her pleasant visit, and said she was sending me a bottle of English embrocation to rub on my bruises after skating; that it was wonderful stuff, and she was sure I would like it; and that it cost two marks, and would I send stamps. I pondered long over this. Was it a parting hit, intended as revenge for our having laughed at her? Was she personally interested in the sale of embrocation? Or was it merely Minora's idea of a graceful return for my hospitality? As for bruises, nobody who skates decently regards it as a bruise-producing exercise, and whenever there were any they were all on Minora; but she did happen to turn round once, I remember, just as I was in the act of tumbling down for the first and only time, and her delight was but thinly veiled by her excessive solicitude and sympathy. I sent her the stamps, received the bottle, and resolved to let her drop out of my life; I had been a good Samaritan to her at the request of my friend, but the best of Samaritans resents the offer of healing oil for his own use. But why waste a thought on Minora at Easter, the real beginning of the year in defiance of calendars. She belongs to the winter that is past, to the darkness that is over, and has no part or lot in the life I shall lead for the next six months. Oh, I could dance and sing for joy that the spring is here! What a resurrection of beauty there is in my garden, and of brightest hope in my heart! The whole of this radiant Easter day I have spent out of doors, sitting at first among the windflowers and celandines, and then, later, walking with the babies to the

Hirschwald, to see what the spring had been doing there; and the afternoon was so hot that we lay a long time on the turf, blinking up through the leafless branches of the silver birches at the soft, fat little white clouds floating motionless in the blue. We had tea on the grass in the sun, and when it began to grow late, and the babies were in bed, and all the little wind-flowers folded up for the night, I still wandered in the green paths, my heart full of happiest gratitude. It makes one very humble to see oneself surrounded by such a wealth of beauty and perfection anonymously lavished, and to think of the infinite meanness of our own grudging charities, and how displeased we are if they are not promptly and properly appreciated. I do sincerely trust that the benediction that is always awaiting me in my garden may by degrees be more deserved, and that I may grow in grace, and patience, and cheerfulness, just like the happy flowers I so much love.

We do hope that you have enjoyed reading this large print book.

Did you know that all of our titles are available for purchase?

We publish a wide range of high quality large print books including:
Romances, Mysteries, Classics
General Fiction
Non Fiction and Westerns

Special interest titles available in large print are:
The Little Oxford Dictionary
Music Book
Song Book
Hymn Book
Service Book

Also available from us courtesy of Oxford University Press:
Young Readers' Dictionary
(large print edition)
Young Readers' Thesaurus
(large print edition)

For further information or a free brochure, please contact us at:
Ulverscroft Large Print Books Ltd.,
The Green, Bradgate Road, Anstey,
Leicester, LE7 7FU, England.
Tel: (00 44) 0116 236 4325
Fax: (00 44) 0116 234 0205

THF ADVENTURES OF MR. VERDANT GREEN

Cuthbert Bede

Young Mr. Verdant Green has tallied up eighteen years of unobjectionable existence at home with his sisters, comfortably insulated from the horrors of public school and the tyranny of sporting activities. But when Mr. Larkyns, local rector and Verdant's tutor, persuades Mr. Green Senior that his student is sorely in need of a little worldly experience, the callow Verdant is dispatched to Oxford for matriculation. As the innocent lamb embarks upon the odyssey of university life with characteristic trusting confidence, he finds himself gambolling into a den of wolves . . .